ANNE MATHER

Brittle Bondage

Harlequin Books

TORONTO • NEW YORK • LONDON
AMSTERDAM • PARIS • SYDNEY • HAMBURG
STOCKHOLM • ATHENS • TOKYO • MILAN
MADRID • WARSAW • BUDAPEST • AUCKLAND

ISBN 0-373-11722-1

BRITTLE BONDAGE

Copyright © 1994 by Anne Mather.

First North American Publication 1995.

Printed in U.S.A.

CHAPTER ONE

RACHEL poured herself a second cup of coffee, and tried not to be aware that her daughter was scowling at her across the width of the pine kitchen table. The postman had just been, so she could distract herself by pretending to study the bills and circulars that made their regular flight through her letterbox. Well, only one bill this morning, she saw with some relief, running her thumb under the flap of the plain brown envelope. Her eyes widened at the sum the electricity company was demanding, and she made a mental note to ask Daisy to be more economical in her use of lights and heating in future. Her daughter seemed to think it was perfectly natural to turn on every utility in the house as soon as she got home. Rachel had lost count of the number of times she had gone into Daisy's bedroom and found the television running in her absence. She couldn't even take a shower without leaving sound and vision on.

'You're not really going to marry him, are you, Mum?'

Abandoning the sullen silence she had maintained all through breakfast, Daisy propped her elbows on the table and assumed a pleading look. Evidently she had decided that silence would get her nowhere. A more constructive approach was needed, and she didn't have a lot of time.

'Aren't you going to be late?' Rachel responded obliquely, unwilling to get into another argument, when there was no time to pursue it. 'Oh, and remember to take your trainers out of the bathroom. It's just as well they weren't muddy. The last time you went running——'

'Mum!' Daisy's tone was urgent now. 'You can't just not talk about it.' She paused. 'If you are thinking of marrying Mr Barrass, don't you think I should be asked

5

my opinion? I don't want to go and live at that gloomy old place. I like living here. This is our home.'

'I know that,' Rachel sighed. 'But, unfortunately, we can't always do what we want. Besides, this house is too big for just the two of us, Daisy. And obviously Simon can't move in with us.'

'Why can't he?'

'You know why.' Rachel picked up her cup and carried it to the sink. 'Kingsmead isn't just Simon's home. It's a working farm.' She took a breath. 'And in any case, this house belongs to your father. I don't think he'd be too enthusiastic about another man moving in.'

Daisy hunched her shoulders. 'Have you told Daddy what you're going to do?'

'No.' Rachel turned away and ran some hot water into the sink. She had wondered if Daisy might have mentioned Simon on her last visit with her father, but evidently Daisy had hoped that if she didn't mention it, it might all go away.

'Why not?'

Rachel steeled herself not to make some comment she might later regret, and turned back to her daughter. 'Daisy, we can't talk about this any more now. I suggest you go and wash your hands and collect your school bag. The bus will be here soon, and you don't want to miss it.'

Daisy sniffed. 'I don't care,' she muttered, making no attempt to do as she had been told. At nearly nine years of age, she was just beginning to show some independence, and Rachel thought it was a pity she had taken a dislike to Simon before she'd really had a chance to get to know him.

'Go and get ready now,' she ordered, suppressing the impulse to try and reason with her once again. And, although Daisy still looked mutinous, she responded to the tone of her mother's voice. But, it was obviously going to take some time to convince her that moving to Kingsmead would be best for all of them. Yet Daisy needed a father, and Simon was an ideal candidate for the job.

And, thinking of Daisy's father reminded Rachel of the other unwelcome task she had to do today. At some point, she was going to have to ring Ben and tell him what she intended to do. And ask for a divorce, she acknowledged tensely. She'd never thought she'd be the first to say that.

Daisy came back into the room wearing her navy school coat and carrying her duffel bag. Whatever happened to satchels? thought Rachel ruefully, realising anew how her daughter was growing up. When she was her age, she'd been considered a child and nothing more. Daisy was a young adult, with all the doubts and hangups of an adolescent.

'Ready?' Rachel tried to instil some optimism into her voice, but Daisy was in no mood to respond to it.

'As if you care,' she mumbled, digging into her pockets for the fingerless gloves she'd brought back from London on her last visit. 'Oh, Miss Gregory asked me to give you this,' she added, discovering a slip of paper advertising for helpers for a jumble sale there was to be held at the school. 'As you helped last year, she thought you might want to help again. I told her you'd probably be too busy, what with Mr Barrass and everything, but Miss Gregory said to tell you anyway.'

Rachel's mouth turned down at the corners. She didn't believe for one moment that Daisy had been discussing her affairs with her teacher. Particularly not anything that involved Simon Barrass. As with her father, Daisy chose to bury her head in the sand and hope the problem would go away. She was just trying to provoke her mother, and it was simpler to play along.

'Oh? What did Miss Gregory say to that?' Rachel enquired now, and had the doubtful privilege of seeing her daughter's face suffuse with colour.

'I don't remember,' muttered Daisy sulkily, going into the hall and peering out of the window. 'Here's the bus. I can't talk now. I've got to go.'

Rachel kissed her daughter goodbye and watched as Daisy ran down the path, and climbed aboard the yellow minibus, which would take her to her private school in Cheltenham. There was a primary school in the next village, but it had been Ben's idea to send Daisy to Lady's Mount Academy and, as he was paying, Rachel had found it difficult to object. Besides, around the time Daisy was starting school, there had been rumours that the school in nearby Lower Morton was going to close. The fact that it hadn't, yet, was no surety that it wouldn't in the future. And Daisy was happy at Lady's Mount, even if it was going to be harder to get her there once they had moved to Kingsmead.

Closing the door, Rachel paused a moment to look around the pleasant entrance hall of the house. Panelled in oak, with exposed beams and an inglenook fireplace, it had been the first thing that had attracted them to the house seven years ago. And, even after everything that had happened, Rachel knew she would miss the place terribly when they moved. It was such a friendly house, warm and south-facing, with plenty of room for the expanding family they had planned when they came to live here. Now, she and Daisy rattled around like peas in the many spacious rooms, and for all her many misgivings, it was time they moved on.

Refusing to get maudlin about it, Rachel dried the few breakfast dishes she and Daisy had used, and then ran up the dog-leg staircase to put on a little make-up. She didn't use much—just a touch of eyeshadow and a smear of blusher. And a coat of amber lipstick, to go with the tawny highlights in her hair.

A door opened from the stairs, at the point where the small landing created the right angle. Beyond the door was a room set into the eaves of the adjoining garage, with a partially sloping roof, and wide dormer windows.

Although she didn't really have the time to waste, Rachel opened the door on to what had been Ben's study, and stood for a few moments looking in. When Ben moved his desk out, she had moved a work table in, intending, at that time, to use the study as a sewing-room in future. But she never had. Such sewing as she did do, she did in the family-room downstairs, and, apart from looking emptier than it used to do, the room was much the same as when Ben had worked there. His books were gone as well, of course, and the hi-fi system he'd sometimes played while he was working. Now it was just a junk-room really, not an office at all. There was no lingering trace of Ben's occupancy. A conscious choice on her behalf.

All the same, she knew she would find it a wrench parting with the house. Although Ben had insisted she live in it after the separation, she was fond of the place. But it was still Ben's house. She was still Ben's wife. And that was something else she had to deal with. As Simon had said, the sooner the better.

A watery sun appeared as she was leaving. So far it had been a wet spring, and although the daffodils and crocuses were out they were all waterlogged in their beds. At the weekend, she'd have to make an effort to prune the roses, she thought, passing the prickly patch of bushes on her way to the garage. And the greenhouse needed cleaning, if she hoped to grow any decent tomatoes this year.

Except that she wouldn't be cultivating the greenhouse this year, she reminded herself. Simon had suggested she should move into one of the tied cottages on the farm, while they were waiting for her divorce to be final and they could get married. It was more sensible, he said, pointing out that it took him a good twenty minutes to get to Upper Morton, where she lived, and a further twenty minutes to get back.

'Just think of all the petrol I'll save, when I can walk home after seeing you!' he had exclaimed, and although he had smiled when he said it, she didn't really know if he was serious or not.

In any event, there were other advantages as well. Not least the fact that she wouldn't have the upkeep of this house making a drain on her wages. Simon had said she could live at the farm rent-free, and she couldn't deny that lately keeping their heads above water had become a constant strain.

She could have asked Ben to increase her allowance— the allowance she got for Daisy, and which was far more generous than the upkeep of one small girl warranted— but she had her pride. If she could have afforded it, she would have supported Daisy herself. But it wasn't fair to expect Daisy to suffer, just because her mother had some misguided desire for independence. It was Ben who had betrayed his family; Ben who had destroyed their marriage. He deserved to pay something for the privilege. The fact that what he did pay her hardly made a dent in his small change shouldn't concern her. Until now they had had the house, and just enough to live on. If Ben felt any emotion at her changing circumstances, it should be one of relief. After all, it would be to his advantage if she didn't have to rely on him for anything.

But, as she drove through the stone gateposts that marked the boundaries of Wychwood, Rachel couldn't help the unwilling thought that Ben was unlikely to see it that way. He was amazingly possessive when it came to his daughter, and she doubted he'd take kindly to the thought that some other man was going to take his place in their lives. He hadn't put up any opposition when she had applied for custody of Daisy, and he had been charitably disposed to allow her to make what visitation rights she thought fit. But that had been two years ago, when, so far as Rachel was concerned, there had been no one else on the horizon. How Ben would react to the news of Simon's entry into their lives was anyone's guess, but Rachel doubted he would applaud the fact that she was upsetting Daisy's life once again.

Well, that wasn't her fault, she told herself now, turning out of Stoneberry Lane and driving swiftly through the village. Upper Morton was the twin of its rival, Lower Morton, and when she and Ben had first seen the two villages they had been hard pressed to choose between them. They had just known they wanted to live in this part of Gloucestershire, and finding the house of their dreams had seemed to seal their fate.

And it had, thought Rachel ruefully, though definitely not in the way they had envisaged. After all, they had been happy in the beginning. Ecstatically so, considering the gamble they had taken, when they didn't always know how they were going to pay the mortgage.

But it had been so different from the flat they had lived in in London, with a garden for Daisy to play in, and lots of room for Ben to work without being disturbed. Room for their family to grow, too, although that hadn't happened. Would things have turned out differently if she had been able to have another baby? Would Elena Dupois have come into their lives, if Rachel hadn't decided to go back to work?

It wasn't as if they had needed the money. By that time, Ben had had his first advance on the novel he had written about the Falklands War. His agent was already talking about overseas sales and film rights, and Ben was writing furiously, completing his second manuscript.

Rachel had sometimes wondered if the enormity of Ben's success had in any way contributed to her proven inadequacies. If his first attempt to write a political thriller hadn't had such immediate appeal, would she have examined her own defeats so minutely? She hadn't been envious of Ben, but she had felt inferior to him. A feeling she had never experienced when he was a journalist, working for a national daily, and she had been straight out of art school, training with one of the larger auction houses in the West End.

It was pointless going over all the old arguments at this stage. Pointless remembering how shattered she had been when she had miscarried for the second time. There was nothing wrong with her, the doctor had assured her. His suggestion was that she should wait a few months and then try again. But Rachel had refused to do it. She had been too distressed, too drained, too afraid of what it was doing to her own self-esteem to risk another pregnancy. When Ben attempted to persuade her, she accused him of having no feelings; when she told him she wanted to find a job, he accused her of being jealous.

She supposed that was the turning point in their marriage. Ben assumed that being his wife was not enough for her, and she had no convincing answer. She couldn't explain her feelings. Not to his satisfaction, anyway. A yawning rift opened between them, and Ben was left to draw his own conclusions.

And that was when Elena Dupois came on the scene. Obviously, Ben couldn't look after Daisy while Rachel was at work, so they advertised for an au pair. Elena answered the advertisement. She had been working for a family in Cheltenham who were moving away, and as she wanted to stay in the district she was able to take up the post immediately.

Rachel's lips tightened. She supposed she should have seen the writing on the wall. Elena was younger than she was and prettier than she was, and from the very beginning she hadn't tried to hide her admiration for Ben. It was 'Monsieur Ben says this' and 'Monsieur Ben says that' until Rachel wanted to scream that 'Monsieur Ben' wasn't the only person who lived in the house.

But she was good with Daisy, and, as her daughter was doing now, Rachel had tended to bury her head in the sand. She hadn't wanted to see what was happening under her very eyes. She hadn't wanted to believe that Ben was cheating on her with the doe-eyed French girl.

Until that morning when she had arrived home unexpectedly and found them in what could only be described as 'compromising circumstances'. Even now, two years later, Rachel could still feel the cold horror she had felt then. She'd felt sick, nauseated; she'd wanted to run away and hide, and come back later, when she could pretend it had never happened. But, instead, she'd disgraced herself completely by throwing up all over the bathroom floor. Her ignominy had been complete when it was Ben himself who cleaned her up and guided her into their bedroom, so that she could lie down for a while. With only a towel to cover his nakedness, she remembered. It was only later she had decided she wanted to kill him.

Of course, he'd tried to talk to her, to explain that if Elena was pregnant—as she claimed—it was nothing to do with him. He'd blamed Elena—Rachel—anyone but himself. It wasn't what she'd thought, he'd yelled, losing his temper completely when she'd refused to listen, but if he *had* decided to have an affair—which he hadn't, he insisted—she'd have only herself to blame.

Which had been a bitter reminder that it was months since they had made love. Afraid of getting pregnant again, Rachel had been unwilling to take any chances. Even his suggestion that she should leave the precautions to him had met with a tearful refusal. In her misery, Rachel had insisted on keeping him at a distance, and perhaps it was her fault that he'd found solace with someone else.

Ben had moved out the next week. Rachel didn't know that until later. She had gathered up a few of her belongings, and her daughter, and left for London that afternoon. She and Daisy—who had happily regarded the trip as an unexpected holiday—had spent the next two weeks with Rachel's widowed mother in Kensington. Rachel had used the time to think and plan for the future, only returning to Wychwood when she had been sure of what she wanted to do.

What she had not expected was that Ben should have moved out. After all, the house was his. She had contributed nothing to it, and he had every right to stay there. On top of which, it was obviously much too big for her to maintain on the salary she got from Mr Caldwell, the local antiquarian. Daisy would miss it, it was true, but in Rachel's opinion they had no choice but to sell.

However, in this instance, Ben had proved decidedly obdurate. After a letter from her solicitors, laying out the situation as she saw it, he had arrived at Wychwood one cold November afternoon, and proceeded to inform her that if she chose to obstruct the arrangements he was making for his daughter's future, he would oppose the order she was making to obtain custody of the child. He had no intention, he said, of allowing her misplaced bitterness to foul up his daughter's life, as it had fouled up his own. She would stay at Wychwood, because that was what he wanted, and he would maintain its upkeep, just as he had done in the past. She was a selfish, self-centred woman, he had added, but he was prepared to accept that Daisy would probably be happier with her.

Privately, Rachel had thought that it probably suited him not to have the responsibility for a seven-year-old. To all intents and purposes, he was a free man; a wealthy man, moreover, whose reputation as a writer and an historian was growing in leaps and bounds. What she couldn't understand was why he didn't want a divorce. In his position, she was sure she would have.

But perhaps it had suited him, too, to have an absentee wife and daughter in the background. On the one hand, it proved his masculinity, if any proof were needed. And, on the other, it prevented him from getting embroiled in any other serious relationships. There had been several women mentioned in connection with him in articles she had read since they separated. Though Elena Dupois had never figured in any of these articles. He had evidently lost interest in her once the novelty of having sex with a girl half his age had worn off, and the baby she had presumably had was never mentioned.

Perhaps it had been adopted. Perhaps he was maintaining it and Elena somewhere else. Rachel told herself she didn't want to know. As far as she was concerned, that period of her life was over.

Rachel had sometimes wondered what Daisy really thought of their separation. The explanation she had been given—that Mummy and Daddy had each decided they needed more time to themselves—had sufficed when Daisy was younger, but latterly she had begun to question the reasons why they chose to live apart. This had been especially evident since Simon Barrass had come into their lives. Daisy made no secret of her dislike for the burly farmer, and she had even gone so far as to ask why, if her mother needed a man's company now, she didn't just ask her father to come back and live with them.

Sometimes, Rachel wished Daisy had been older when she and Ben split up. It would have been so much easier if she could have explained what had happened, and why the separation had taken place. As it was, she was obliged to deal in euphemisms and half-truths, balancing the need for honesty with her daughter's fragile expectations.

Which brought her back to the prospect she still faced of telling Ben what she planned to do. Had she really hoped Daisy might have prepared the ground for her? After all, Simon had been around for some considerable time, and Daisy spent one weekend every month with her father.

The arrangement had been worked out by Ben, of course. Every four weeks—and more frequently during school holidays—a car arrived to collect Daisy and her belongings from Wychwood, and transport her to Ben's luxurious town-house in Elton Square. Usually there was a uniformed nanny in attendance, who took care of the little girl's personal needs while she was staying with her father. And kept her out of his way, on those occasions when he had guests, or went out to dine, thought Rachel ruefully. These days, Ben's company was much in demand at literary gatherings, Press launches and the like. Rachel knew this, because she still cut out every

article she found about him from newspapers or
magazines. It was a fruitless exercise, she knew, and one
which she told herself she was only doing for Daisy's
sake. But the fact remained that she still felt an unwilling twinge of pride every time she saw his name in
print. After all, she had recognised his talent even before
he'd recognised it himself. It had been her idea that he
should take a chance and give up his regular job, and
try for the thing he most wanted. That he had been so
successful was all due to him, of course, but without her
encouragement he might never have taken the plunge.

She was so engrossed with her thoughts that she almost
drove past the small antiques shop where she worked.
Mr Caldwell's establishment was an attractive double-
fronted dwelling that sat squarely in the High Street,
with a post office and general dealers on one side of
him, and the doctor's surgery on the other. With its bow
windows and leaded panes, it invited inspection, and Mr
Caldwell always made sure they had some unusual item
in the window to encourage would-be customers to come
inside. At present, an eighteenth-century tripod table had
pride of place, with a Chinese ormolu clock set squarely
on its mahogany surface. Mr Caldwell liked to create a
gathering of matching pieces together, which was why
there was a pair of Queen Anne chairs standing at either
side of the table, though it was obvious to an experienced eye that the chairs were not in the same class as
the table. Rachel had learned that an experienced eye
was worth more than a dozen reference books, and it
was her aptitude for seeking out a bargain that had persuaded Mr Caldwell to take her on in the first place.

Now, Rachel parked her Volkswagen at the back of
the shop, and, after making sure it was locked, she
crossed the yard to the rear entrance. Mr O'Shea, who
restored many of the scratched and damaged items of
furniture Mr Caldwell bought to a convincing orig-
inality, was already at work in the warehouse that ad-
joined the shop. A cheery individual, he always had a

smile and a friendly word for Rachel, and today was no exception.

'Spring is on its way,' he announced, with sturdy conviction. 'So why are you looking so troubled, lassie? That old besom hasn't been complaining again, has he?'

'Oh, no.' Rachel cast a guilty glance towards the front of the building, but her lips twitched in spite of herself. 'And you shouldn't say such things, Mr O'Shea. Do you want to get me into trouble?'

'Away with ye, lassie. He'll not be parting with you in a hurry. You're too valuable to him, Rachel, and that's a fact. You've got a good eye. Aren't I always telling you so?'

'You've got the gift of the gab,' retorted Rachel drily, admiring the finish he was putting to a figured walnut chest. 'Is this that Queen Anne chest that Cyril found in Worcester? It's beautiful. You've done a lovely job on it.'

'Ah, so there you are at last, Rachel.'

Her employer's voice put an end to her conversation with Mr O'Shea, and, following Mr Caldwell into the cramped passageway that led through to the front of the shop, Rachel reflected, not for the first time, that any fire inspector who examined this place would probably close it down as a fire hazard. Every spare inch of space was covered with crates and boxes of china, while framed portraits and uncut canvases were a constant threat to her legs and ankles.

But, for all that, Rachel loved her job. She loved the smell and the touch of old things, and, it was true, she felt she did have a certain aptitude for the work. The arts degree she had left college with might have seemed important at the time, but it was the innate ability she possessed to recognise shape and colour, and a memory for detail, that had impressed her present employer. In the five years she had worked for Cyril Caldwell, she had proved her worth again and again, which was why she knew he wouldn't be pleased to hear she was planning to get married again. Cyril liked to feel he had her whole and undivided attention.

Rachel was wondering whether she ought to break the news to him now, before it filtered down through the grapevine that operated so efficiently between the villages, when Mr Caldwell spoke.

'I have to go out,' he said, leading the way into the showroom. 'I've just heard that there's a group of Meissen figurines among all that junk they're selling out at Romanby, and I want to get there and take a look at them before Hector Grant gets his hands on them all. You can manage here, can't you? I thought you might unpack that box of glassware, if you have the time. And there's some discrepancy in those figures Parkers sent us. You might have a look at those, too.'

Rachel hesitated. 'Well——' This might not be the most appropriate time, but she wondered if it wouldn't be easier on her to give Cyril her news when he didn't have the time to argue. 'I did want to have a word with you——'

'Later, Rachel, hmm?' But it wasn't really a question. He was already consulting the watch he kept in his waistcoat pocket, mentally calculating the time it would take him to get to Romanby Court, and checking that he had his cheque-book and catalogue in a safe place.

'OK.'

Rachel decided not to push it. There was no guarantee that her news wouldn't delay him anyway, and she had no wish to be the excuse he would give if he didn't happen to acquire any of the Meissen figures.

'Good, good.'

He made his way to the shop door, a slightly shabby figure in his tweed suit and battered felt hat. But one of the first things he had taught her was that it was unwise to go to an auction looking too affluent. Dealers were a canny breed, and the less successful you looked, the more successful you were likely to be. He had also told her that you had to stay close to the competition. Many articles were sold, not because they were intrinsically valuable, but because someone liked the look of them. Antique dealing was a buyer's market. The secret was to create a demand for something, and then sell it at the highest price you could get.

The doorbell chimed as he went out, and Rachel expelled her breath on a rueful sigh as she went to watch him get into his car. Like the man himself, it was shabby, too, an old Peugeot estate car of doubtful vintage. Cyril had had the car as long as Rachel could remember, and she felt a twinge of affection as he pulled away from the kerb. He might be old and cantankerous at times, but he had supported her when she'd needed it most. Which was an unwelcome reminder of that call she had to make, and, after watching Cyril disappear out of sight, she went back to her desk.

CHAPTER TWO

IT FELT odd to be punching in the buttons that made up Ben's London phone number. Irritating, too, that she didn't even need to consult her address book to remind herself what they were. She assumed it was because she had used the number fairly often in the early days of their separation. After she'd been convinced by Ben's attitude that he wouldn't deal with her solicitors.

Still, it didn't make it any easier to make the call, and she was annoyed to find her hands were trembling. Dear God, she thought, what did she expect him to do, for heaven's sake? Appear like a wrathful genie out of the mouthpiece? She was only asking to terminate something that had been terminated in everything but name for the past two years. She knew nothing about Ben's life any more, and he knew nothing about hers. It was time they had a formal severance of their marriage. Daisy might not like it, but Rachel had a life of her own to lead.

The phone seemed to ring an inordinately long period of time before it was picked up, and Rachel was just beginning to think he must be away when it was answered.

'Yes?' It was a woman's voice, and Rachel's nerves tightened. 'This is Knightsbridge...' She gave the number. 'Who is this, please?'

Rachel wanted to hang up. She wanted to make some obscene comment, and slam down the phone. But she didn't. What did it matter to her who answered Ben's phone? she chided herself grimly. It wasn't as if she wanted a reconciliation. Actually she wanted anything but.

All the same, she resented the offhand tone in the woman's voice. As if her call had interrupted something crucial, and the woman had been told to get rid of her as quickly as possible. She hadn't even said anything, and she was already being made to feel a nuisance.

She sighed. This was silly. She was getting paranoid over the call. The woman didn't know who she was yet. She could be the Prime Minister's secretary, or even the Prime Minister himself. Until she indentified herself, how could they know?

'Um—who am I speaking to?' she asked, realising she was still on the defensive when it was too late to do anything about it. But she was loath to give her name to one of Ben's bimbos. If he wanted to know who it was, he should have answered the phone himself.

'I'm—Karen Simpson, Mr Leeming's secretary,' responded the woman, after only a momentary hesitation. 'Do you wish to speak to Mr Leeming? If you'll give me your name, I'll see if he's available.'

His secretary! Rachel's lips twisted. Well, she'd heard it called worse names. Ben had never had a secretary; not to her knowledge. And she was sure Daisy would have mentioned it, if there had been another woman around.

'I think you'll find he'll speak to me,' she said, aware that she wasn't being very polite, but incapable of reacting any differently. 'I'm Mrs Leeming. Mr Leeming's *wife*!' She emphasised the relationship with childish defiance. 'Perhaps if he has a minute you could ask him to come to the phone.'

'Mr Leeming's wife!' Clearly, the woman was impressed. Or was she simply surprised? Rachel wondered ruefully. She wasn't handling this in a very mature way, and she wished she could ring off and start all over again.

'Yes, Mr Leeming's wife,' she repeated now, with less emphasis. 'Is Mr Leeming there? It is rather important.'

'Just a minute, Mrs Leeming.'

The phone went dead. Though not quite dead, Rachel amended, winding the cord nervously round her finger. Evidently Ben had one of those phones with a cut-out button, ideal for monitoring unwanted callers. Rachel wondered if he had one in his bedroom, and then despised herself for the thought. His private arrangements were nothing to do with her any more.

'Rachel?'

The voice in her ear was suddenly uncomfortably familiar. It might have been months, years even, since they had had a conversation, but that dark, mellow tone was unmistakable.

'Hello, Ben.' Rachel wished she had something to lubricate her dry throat. 'I'm sorry if I'm disturbing you.'

Now why had she said that? she wondered impatiently. The accusation behind her words was clearly audible. Why couldn't she have just launched into the reason why she was calling, instead of giving him a chance to make some clever retort?

'I can stand the break,' he responded shortly, and if that was a *double entendre* she didn't have time to acknowledge it. 'What is it? Has something happened to Daisy?'

She supposed she should have realised that Ben was bound to associate her reasons for calling with his daughter, but just for a moment she felt a spurt of resentment that this should be so. She had a life, too, she wanted to exclaim loudly. Not everything in her world had to revolve around Daisy.

But once again, common sense won out over her reckless inclinations. And she wondered suddenly why she was making this call. She could have written to Ben just as well. But he was on the line now, and she was committed. If she didn't tell him the truth, she'd be a coward as well as a fool.

'Daisy's fine,' she replied quickly, mentally rummaging through her recent altercations with her daughter for something positive to relate. 'She seems to be enjoying school, and she's made a lot of friends, as I'm sure she's told you. Oh, and I've been asked to help out at the jumble sale again. It's a week on Saturday. Last year, I ran one of the stalls.'

'Am I invited?'

'What?' For a moment, Rachel was too shocked by his response to remember exactly why she had chosen to tell him about the jumble sale. Then, 'Oh—oh, no. That's not why I was ringing. Um—we don't visit the school together, do we? We agreed that we wouldn't encroach on one another's——'

'All right.' Ben's voice held a note of censure now. 'I should have known better than to think you wanted us to appear as a family again. So—if you're not ringing about Daisy, what are you ringing about, Rachel? I don't know if Karen told you, but I am rather busy.'

Karen! Rachel controlled her anger with an effort. 'Your secretary,' she said sweetly, though she feared he would hear the acid in her tone. 'I didn't know you had a secretary, Ben. Daisy never mentioned her. Is she new?'

'What's it to you?' Ben could be obstructive, too, and she felt her nails dig into her palms. 'Come on, Rachel, I'm sure you're not ringing to check on my staff appointments. Did you decide to accept my offer of an increase in your allowance? I can backdate it, if you like. I dare say a lump sum would come in handy.'

'You don't make *me* an allowance,' retorted Rachel hotly, furious that he should immediately think she was short of money. The fact that she usually was was immaterial. She refused to take anything from him that was not specifically targeted for Daisy.

'As you like.' Ben sounded bored now. 'But if you're not ringing about Daisy and you're not ringing about money, what do you want? The last time I tried to have a conversation with you, you informed me we had nothing to say to one another.'

Rachel sighed. 'Look,' she said, trying to sound as reasonable as her intentions had been before she picked up the receiver, 'I didn't call you to have an argument. I'm sorry if I've called at an inconvenient time, but I wasn't sure I'd find you in this evening. Um—as a matter of fact, I probably should have written to you. Solicitors prefer these things down on paper, don't they? Just so there's no mistakes. Only you wouldn't deal with Mr Cockcroft before, and before contacting him, I thought I should warn you. I mean, I'm sure we can be adult about this. I surely didn't intend for us to get cross with one another. I know you won't believe this, but I was only trying to be polite——'

'Hold it! Hold it right there!' Ben broke into her breathless monologue in harsh tones. 'For God's sake, Rachel, what the—hell—are you talking about?'

The hesitation before the word 'hell' warned her of his dwindling patience. And she was fairly sure that if Miss Simpson hadn't been on hand he wouldn't have been so scrupulous. She was familiar with Ben's sometimes colourful use of the language, and the mildness of the epithet in no way detracted from its force.

'Divorce,' she blurted hurriedly, before his arrogance and her timidity defeated her again. 'I want a divorce, Ben. I—I've met someone else, and we want to get married.'

There was total silence after her announcement. If it wasn't for the fact that Rachel already knew that the phone had a cut-out, she'd have been quite prepared to believe he had hung up on her. But that wasn't Ben's way. For all his faults, he had never been one to back off from a challenge. And this was a challenge, she realised belatedly. To his authority, if nothing else.

The silence stretched, and then, just when her nerves had reached screaming point, he said calmly, 'I think we need to talk.'

Rachel breathed a sigh of relief. 'Oh, I agree,' she said, swallowing the sudden flood of saliva that had filled her mouth at his words. 'That's why I'm ringing. I thought if we could arrange the details now, and you could make an appointment to see your solicitor——'

'No.'

The denial after she had felt such an overwhelming sense of relief was shattering. 'What do you mean, no?'

'I mean you've misunderstood me.'

Rachel blinked, totally confused now. 'You're saying I can't have a divorce?'

'No——'

'Then what?' She recovered a little of her composure and struggled to sound reasonable. 'I think you should say what you mean, Ben. Like you, I have work to do, too.'

And as if to endorse the point, the door of the shop opened at that moment, its bell chiming delicately round the elegantly furnished showroom. A man had come into the shop, a man of middle height, with square, sturdy shoulders, and a well-muscled, solid build. He was wearing tweeds, and a pair of green boots, his thinning fair hair hidden beneath a buttoned corduroy cap.

It was Simon Barrass, and Rachel, who would have normally been delighted to see him, viewed his presence now with a nervous eye. It wasn't that she didn't want him here, she told herself, shifting the receiver from one ear to the other. She just didn't want him to interpret her tolerance of Ben's attitude as intimidation. Having heard the story of what had happened from Rachel, Simon was, naturally enough, resentful of the pain Ben had put her through. He had already threatened to deal with him personally, if her soon-to-be-ex-husband made things difficult for her. And, although she wasn't entirely convinced that Simon, burly though he was, could threaten Ben, she didn't want their marriage to begin in such a way. Apart from anything else, Daisy would never forgive Simon if he hurt her father. And as for accepting him . . .

'Look, we can't talk now,' she declared hurriedly, as the urge to avoid Simon's learning who she was talking to overcame her desire to get things settled with Ben. Catching Simon's eye, she gave him what she hoped was a welcoming smile. 'Um—can I ring you later? I'm afraid I've got a customer.'

'Have you?'

Ben's response was heavily ironic, and she wished she had the freedom to tell him exactly what she thought of him. But until the divorce was finalised it was unwise to antagonise him. And she had delivered quite a broadside. Perhaps it was as well to give him time to absorb the news.

'Yes,' she said now, submitting to the rather wet kiss Simon was bestowing on her ear with some misgivings. 'I won't be a minute,' she assured him softly, covering the mouthpiece as she did so. Then, 'Will that be convenient?' she enquired in a businesslike tone, as her fiancé chose to wedge his hips on the desk beside her.

'OK, Rachel.' To her relief, Ben seemed to accept her explanation. 'Oh, give my love to Daisy, won't you? Tell her Daddy says he'll see her soon.'

'I will.'

Taking no more chances, Rachel put down the receiver, only realising as she looked up into Simon's curious face that she hadn't even said goodbye. Oh, lord, she wondered, had he been able to hear Ben's last few words?

'Awkward customer?' he asked, arching brows only a couple of shades darker than his hair, and Rachel gazed at him uncertainly, not sure how to answer him.

'Not—not really,' she offered, casting her eyes down and pretending to rummage in the drawer for some papers. She was sure her face must be scarlet. She wasn't a practised liar. And she wasn't entirely sure why she was prevaricating anyway. It wasn't as if Ben had refused to discuss a divorce. She pulled out what she had supposedly been looking for, and assumed a bland expression. 'You're an unexpected visitor.'

'But not an unwelcome one, I trust?' suggested Simon, smiling, and she breathed a treacherous sigh of relief.

'Not at all,' she said, not altogether truthfully, allowing him to grasp her hand and squeeze it tightly between both of his. 'I just thought you'd be busy, that's all. With all the spring planting and everything.'

'We'd be in a poor state if I was only now beginning the spring planting,' declared Simon reprovingly, massaging her wrist between his palms. 'You've a lot to learn, Rachel, and it's going to be my pleasure to teach you. Now, where is that old codger you work for? I want to ask him a favour.'

'Mr Caldwell?' Rachel was surprised. She wouldn't have thought Simon and Cyril had anything in common.

'Yes, Cyril,' said Simon forcefully, releasing her hand and getting up from the desk. 'I've got to go to Bristol this morning, and I told Mother I was going to take you with me.' He glanced round. 'Now, if you'll just point me in his direction—— '

'He's not here.' Tamping down the indignation she felt at not being asked whether she wanted to go to Bristol with him or not, Rachel got up too, rubbing her hands together. Then, realising it was just a nervous way of drying her sweating palms, she ran them swiftly down the seams of her linen skirt. 'Mr Caldwell,' she explained. 'He's gone to a sale at Romanby. I don't know how long he'll be. Probably several hours at the least.'

'Oh, damn!' Simon's use of epithets was always conservative, but there was no doubting his irritation at this news. 'And I suppose you can't leave the shop, can you? What a nuisance! The sooner you're not dependent on this place for a livelihood, the better!'

Rachel swallowed. So far, this had not been the best day she had ever had, and it was getting no better. 'What do you mean, Simon?' she asked. 'I hope to work for Mr Caldwell for many years to come. I like it here. I like my job. I thought you understood that. I thought you realised how important it is to me.'

Simon blushed now, his fair, good-looking face flushing with unbecoming colour. It made him look both younger and less confident, and Rachel felt a twinge of conscience for reacting as sharply as she had. It was all Ben's fault, she decided, resenting the fact that he was still occupying too large a place in her thoughts. She ought to feel flattered that Simon enjoyed her company so much. After all, he hadn't left Wychwood until nearly midnight last night.

'I do, of course.' He spoke urgently now. 'I didn't mean that I wanted you to give up your job, Rachel. It's just that we get so little time alone together. I'm very fond of Daisy, you know that. But she is inclined to hover over us whenever I'm—at your house.'

Rachel bit her lip. She wanted to defend her daughter, but the truth was Daisy was very possessive whenever Simon was around. It was her way of protecting what she saw as her father's property, and not until she and Ben were divorced would Daisy really accept that their marriage was over.

'It's—difficult, I know,' she conceded, and saw the colour in Simon's face fade a little at her words. 'But we do have time together after Daisy's gone to bed.'

'Mmm.' Simon didn't sound convinced. 'So long as she doesn't feel sick, or want a drink, or discover a spider in the bathroom.'

Rachel had to laugh then. 'She does have a mine of excuses,' she agreed. 'But once Ben and I are divorced...'

'It can't be soon enough for me,' declared Simon, nodding. 'It should be easier then, as you say. Providing your ex-husband doesn't try to maintain too much influence over her. You know, Rachel, it might be an idea to make an alteration to the custody order to the effect that you'll take control of Daisy's schooling. It's obviously not going to be practical to keep her at Lady's Mount after you've moved to Kingsmead. There's a perfectly adequate school in Lower Morton, and when she's eleven——'

'I think we ought to talk about this at some other time, Simon,' Rachel broke in hurriedly, realising that until she had discussed it with Ben there was no way she could make arbitrary judgements. Simon had no idea how her husband would react to any change in his daughter's circumstances, and just because he hadn't jumped down her throat when she broached the subject this morning was no reason to assume he was indifferent to her plans. She'd ring him again this evening, and try and get some definite decision from him. Perhaps after he'd had time to think it over, he'd see it was for the best.

'I suppose you're right.' To her relief, Simon at least seemed prepared to accede to her wishes. Or perhaps he was simply relieved. 'Well, I suppose I'd better go. If you can't come with me, you can't. I'll think of you when I'm sitting in Alberto's, enjoying one of his peppered steaks.'

'Do that.'

Rachel accompanied him to the door of the shop, and allowed him to give her a rather more intimate kiss before taking his leave of her.

'I'll see you tonight,' he said, replacing his cap as he stepped out into the cooler air. 'About seven, hmm?'

'Oh, I——' Rachel struggled to find the words. 'Would you mind if we didn't see one another tonight? I—well, I've got to speak to Ben some time, and—and tonight seems as good a time as any.'

'Without me listening in, do you mean?' he asked drily. 'I suppose that's why you put him off just now.' He paused, and then added pointedly, 'Don't forget to give Daisy his love.'

Rachel's breath escaped with a rush. 'You heard!'

'Well, my hearing is fairly acute, despite my advanced years,' remarked Simon evenly. 'Why didn't you tell me he'd rung you, Rachel? I thought we didn't have any secrets from one another.'

'We don't. And he didn't.' Rachel felt terrible now. 'I rang him. I just—didn't want to involve you, when it wasn't necessary.'

'Everything you do is necessary to me,' retorted Simon, gazing at her with pale possessive eyes. 'But I'll respect your wish to deal with your husband on your own terms. However, if there should be any problem over the divorce——'

'There won't be.' But Rachel crossed her fingers as she said it.

'I hope not.' Simon balled one fist and pressed it into the palm of his other hand. 'It's not as if you want anything from him. You're only finalising something that should have been finalised long ago.'

CHAPTER THREE

IT WAS after six when Rachel and Daisy got home.

Mr Caldwell didn't get back from Romanby until nearly five, and then he insisted on being brought up to date with everything that had happened in his absence. It didn't help that he had imbibed rather too freely in the hospitality tent at the sale, and consequently needed Rachel to repeat everything several times before he grasped what she was saying.

Daisy noticed, of course.

On those occasions when Rachel had to work late, the bus dropped her daughter off at the shop, and Daisy spent the time between her arrival and their leaving either reading, or doing her homework, or chatting with Mr O'Shea. She was a great favourite with the garrulous restorer, and Rachel was immensely grateful to him for making her feel so welcome.

But, as was to be expected, this evening Daisy chose to be a little too forthright in her opinion of Mr Caldwell's behaviour. 'Is he drunk?' she hissed, in the kind of stage-whisper guaranteed to carry to the back of an auditorium, and the elderly antiquarian regarded her with unconcealed dislike.

'If you can't teach that child any better manners than that, then perhaps you ought to find somewhere else for her to stay until you get home from work,' he declared contentiously, and Rachel thought how strange it was that some days just lent themselves to discord. Perhaps this wasn't a good night to ring Ben after all. In the present climate, he was likely to oppose her every suggestion.

'I think you should apologise to Mr Caldwell at once, Daisy,' she said now, putting the question of how she

31

was going to deal with Ben aside for the moment. She wanted no complications with her job to add to her other problems, and although Daisy stared at her with accusing eyes, she recognised an order when she heard one.

'I'm sorry,' she muttered mutinously, and although Mr Caldwell looked as if he would have liked to pursue the vendetta the shrill peal of the phone diverted his attention. And, by the time the call was over, he had forgotten all about chastising Daisy. A situation Rachel had assisted by making sure her daughter kept out of his sight until it was time for them to leave.

Consequently, she was in no mood to contemplate ringing Ben, after she had just watched Daisy demolish a plate of fish fingers and chips. Her own plate was barely touched, and, deciding she deserved some compensation for the day she had had, Rachel rescued a chilled bottle of hock from the fridge. She had put the wine to cool in anticipation of Simon's joining her for supper that evening, but as he wasn't coming now she had no reason to wait before opening it.

Pouring herself a glass, she carried it into the family room, standing in the middle of the floor, surveying these so familiar surroundings. It was the one aspect of her relationship with Simon that didn't fill her with enthusiasm. She would miss this house; she would miss living here. For all its less favourable associations, she had been happy here. It was her home. It had been her home for the past seven years. She couldn't cast it off without some feelings of remorse. And lamenting what might have been if Ben hadn't torn their lives apart...

'Can I watch television, Mummy?'

Rachel turned to find her daughter regarding her from the open doorway, and although her melancholy mood inclined her to be generous, she didn't immediately grant her request.

'Do you remember what happened this afternoon?' she reminded Daisy severely. 'You were rude to Mr

Caldwell, and I said there'd be no television for the next two days.'

'I remember.' Daisy wedged her shoulder against the door.

'Well, then?'

'But it's not fair.'

'It is fair.' Rachel steeled herself against her daughter's mournful expression. 'You know perfectly well you don't make personal comments about anyone. I've already had to speak to you once today about your attitude towards Simon.'

'This is different,' argued Daisy hotly.

'How is it different?'

'Well...' Daisy sniffed. 'You said people who drink shouldn't drive,' she declared, and Rachel sighed.

'So?' But she knew what was coming.

'Well, Mr Caldwell had driven, hadn't he? All the way from Romanby. What if he'd had an accident? What if someone—some child—had been killed?'

Rachel shook her head. 'Nothing happened.'

Daisy rolled her eyes. 'But what if it had?'

'That still doesn't excuse your behaviour.'

Daisy expelled her breath on a noisy sigh. 'But he wasn't supposed to hear!' she protested fiercely, and Rachel had to suppress an unforgivable desire to laugh. Daisy looked so indignant; so frustrated. And, while there had been no excuse for what she'd said, she was only a child. Things seemed so black and white when you were only nearly nine. It wasn't until you were older that you saw the shades between.

All the same...

Rachel was still undecided what she should do, when Daisy pushed herself away from the door, and dragged her feet across the carpet to the window. The curtains were still undrawn, and the bowls of spring bulbs Rachel had planted the previous autumn were reflected in the glass. She watched Daisy as she plucked broodingly at the delicate shoots, thinking how much more like her father she became with each succeeding year. Not just in her looks, though she was going to be tall, like him, and her mop of unruly curls was every bit as dark; but also in temperament: Daisy could be just as moody as her father, if things didn't happen to go her way.

Beyond the windows, it was getting dark, though not as black as it had been in the depths of winter. Already there were signs that the evenings were getting longer, and in another month or two, they'd be able to sit outside after supper. Though not here, Rachel reminded herself yet again. If Simon had his way, they'd be moving to Kingsmead, when Daisy's school broke up for the Easter holidays.

And it was the thought of this, as much as anything, that persuaded Rachel to give in. However much she might tell herself that Daisy had as much to gain from the move as she did, to begin with it wasn't going to be easy for her. For either of them, admitted Rachel honestly. Much as she cared for Simon, living in a cottage at Kingsmead was going to make a big change in all their lives.

'Oh, all right,' she was beginning, 'we'll say no more about it——' but she never got to finish. As she moved towards her daughter, intent on healing the breach that had opened between them, searching headlights swept across the lamplit room. The cutting of a powerful engine left an uneasy silence in its wake, and even before Daisy let out a crow of excitement Rachel sensed instinctively that it wasn't Simon's car.

'It's Daddy! It's Daddy!' cried Daisy, dancing up and down in undisguised delight. She glanced round at her mother, all her previous ills forgotten, and grinned expectantly. 'Did you hear what I said? It's Daddy! Did you know he was coming? Oh—do you think he's going to stay?'

Not if I have anything to do with it, thought Rachel grimly, as her daughter flew past her on her way to open the door. Dear lord, this was all she needed. She should

have known better than to think she could dispose of
Ben with just a phone call.

Torn between the need to gather her scattered de-
fences and the equally potent need to greet Ben as if his
arrival hadn't just plunged her into a state of blind panic,
Rachel emptied the remaining wine in her glass in one
convulsive gulp. She wished now she had chosen brandy
instead of the pale white juice of the grape. She could
have done with something stronger before she saw her
husband again.

And, foolishly, her hand went to her hair, the tawny
brown hair that Ben had always liked her to wear long.
As if it mattered what she looked like, she thought, reassured that the French plait was still in place none the
less. Not that she could compete with the glamorous
women she had seen him escorting around town in the
articles she collected so assiduously. Nor would she want
to, she assured herself impatiently. But at least she hadn't
put on too much weight or gained a lot of grey hairs.

And it wasn't as if she hadn't seen him since that awful
morning when she had found him and Elena together.
In the early days of the separation, he had come back
to the house on several occasions to collect books and
papers he had left behind. He'd always warned her he
was coming, of course, and most times she had made a
point of being out. He had had a key that fitted their
locks in those days. It wasn't until later that she'd had
them changed.

But that was over a year ago now. Recently, their only
contact had been through Daisy. As she remembered this,
she heard his voice in the hall outside and her mouth
went dry. Whatever he had come for, Daisy had invited
him in.

She realised that if she waited any longer he would
find her there, frozen in the middle of the living-room
carpet, clutching her empty wine glass, like a talisman.
So, putting the glass down, she took the necessary steps
to bring her to the door. He was not going to disconcert

her, she told herself fiercely. But her hands were cold and shaking, and there was a feeling of raw apprehension pooling in her stomach.

When she reached the doorway, she paused, steeling herself to face the man who had once been her only reason for living. God, how naïve she had been in those days, she reflected bitterly. However much she loved Simon, he would never have that kind of power over her. No man would. Ever again.

'Hello, Rachel.'

Despite her determination to take control of the situation, Ben beat her to the punch. Even though he had been laughing with Daisy, and fending off her efforts to climb all over him, he still seemed to sense the exact moment when his wife appeared in the doorway. Straightening, he adjured Daisy to behave herself, and swept back his hair with a lazy hand. And, as she met those night-dark eyes, and saw the veiled hostility lurking between the thick fringe of his lashes, Rachel knew in that instant that this was not a conciliatory visit.

'Hello,' she responded, resisting the effort to check that her skirt was straight, and that the hem of her blouse hadn't escaped from her waistband. The skirt was dusty, she knew, after unpacking the china Mr Caldwell had left her with that morning. There might even be a ladder in her tights. If only she'd thought to look.

'How are you?'

His question was perfunctory, and she thought how typical it was that once again Ben should have taken her unawares. He stood there, cool and assured, in a black cashmere sweater and black trousers, totally in control of himself and this conversation. And she was letting him do it. This was her house, dammit, until she moved out anyway. He had no right to come here and treat her like a visitor in her own home.

'I'm fine,' she said now, icily. 'You?'

'Tired,' he admitted carelessly, though there didn't appear to be a tired bone in his lean-muscled body. On the contrary, he looked fit and aggressively masculine, his superior height reminding her what it was like to look up at a man again.

At five feet nine, taller in heels, Rachel was generally on eye-level terms with the men of her acquaintance. Not least Simon, who was inclined to be self-conscious about his lack of height, and encouraged her to wear flat heeled boots and shoes when they went out together.

'Really?' she remarked now, refusing to feel any sympathy for Ben. 'Then I can't imagine why you've driven all this way. I did say I'd ring you later. There was no need for you to make a personal call.'

'Wasn't there?' Ben's mouth had a faintly ironic curve to it. 'Well, I beg to disagree.' He glanced down at Daisy, doing her best to attract his attention. 'Where my daughter's concerned, nothing is too much trouble.'

'She's my daughter, too,' retorted Rachel, and then wished she hadn't allowed him to force her into such a revealing remark. She'd get nowhere here if she let her temper get the better of her. That was obviously why he'd come. Because he knew it would put her on the defensive.

'Aren't you going to offer Daddy a drink?' Daisy protested now, clearly not unaware of the tension between her parents and doing her best to neutralise it. 'Mummy's just opened a bottle of wine,' she told her father innocently. 'I'll get you a glass, shall I? While you and Mummy go and sit down.'

'I don't think——'

'Your father can't drink and drive——'

Rachel and Ben spoke simultaneously, and Daisy looked from one to the other of them with anxious eyes. 'Daddy won't be driving any more tonight, will he?' she asked her mother frowningly. Then, turning to her father, 'You're not driving straight back to London, are you?'

'Not immediately, no.'

Ben looked at Rachel now, and she felt her face turning red. It was typical of him to arrive when he knew Daisy would be there to defend his actions, she thought angrily. If she turned him away now, she'd be a pariah in her daughter's eyes as well.

As well?

'I'm sure your father hasn't come all this way just to see us, darling,' she declared, taking the coward's way out. 'You forget, he used to live here, too. Daddy has friends in the neighbourhood. He's probably planning to visit them.'

'Friends who chose to believe you rather than me,' he countered in a low tone, leaving Daisy to walk past Rachel on his way to the kitchen. He glanced back at her shocked face, his smile at once accusing and mocking. 'You don't mind if I have a drink of water, do you? I am rather thirsty. It's been quite a while since lunch.'

Rachel's breath eased out slowly, but, meeting her daughter's troubled gaze, she knew she'd met her match. She had no earthly reason for denying Ben either a drink of water, or a bed for the night, if that was what he wanted. This was still his house, and her over-reaction to his appearance was hardly beneficial to her cause.

But the trouble was, she thought as she forced a brittle smile for Daisy's benefit and followed him into the kitchen, she didn't want him here. In the past few months, she had succeeded in banishing all memory of her husband from these rooms, and when she was cooking a meal in the kitchen or reading in the cosy snug she no longer saw Ben's image, superimposed across the room. She used to. For weeks, months, maybe even a year or more, she had seen nothing else. She'd never felt relaxed, never felt free of his prevailing presence. But now she did—and he was going to spoil it all again.

But not for long, she reminded herself firmly. Once she and Daisy moved out of this house, there would be nothing to remind them of her ex-husband. Nothing at all.

It was dark now, and although Ben had his back to her as he ran the tap, she could see his reflection in the window above the sink. Was it just her imagination, or did he look a little weary, as he had said? In any event, he was just as arrogant as ever, she told herself fiercely. And just as unscrupulous, if he didn't get his own way.

'Are you hungry?'

It wasn't what she had planned to say, but the words were out, and Daisy gave her a beaming smile. Evidently, she had said the right thing as far as the little girl was concerned. But then, Daisy was the ultimate optimist. She still thought her parents should be civil with one another.

Ben turned, the glass of water he had requested in his hand. 'Is that an enquiry, or just wishful thinking?' he asked drily. 'Don't tell me: I can have some dry bread with the water!'

'The water was your choice,' retorted Rachel shortly, and then, realising she was letting him rile her again, she forced herself to calm down. 'Naturally, if you're hungry, you're welcome to anything we've got.' She mentally catalogued the contents of the fridge, before adding, 'There's some ready-made lasagne, or I could make you a ham sandwich.'

Ben leaned back against the sink unit, regarding her with dark disturbing eyes. It was an intent look, intended to intimidate she was sure. And, despite her best efforts, she couldn't help feeling self-conscious. What was he thinking? she wondered. Was he comparing her plain, homely appearance with the woman he had left behind him in London?

When he took a drink from his glass, and his attention was briefly diverted, Rachel felt as if a solid weight had been lifted from her shoulders. But her relief was short-lived when he set the glass on the drainer, folded his arms, and looked at her again.

'I'm not hungry,' he informed her flatly, casting a disparaging glance at the still-uncleared supper table. Her barely touched meal of fish fingers and chips looked greasy and unappetising, and she wished she'd had warning of his coming so that she could have at least disposed of the plate. 'It doesn't look as if you were hungry either,' he observed. 'Or was the wine more appealing? You ought to be careful, Rachel. Drinking alone can be dangerous.'

Rachel's lips tightened. 'I don't generally drink alone!' she snapped.

'No?' Ben's eyes narrowed slightly, and, as if sensing their conversation was not going as well as she had hoped, Daisy broke in again.

'D'you want to come and see my room, Daddy?' she asked, tugging on his hand. 'I want to show you my computer. It's not as big as yours, but it's ever so good——'

'Later, sweetheart.' Ben allowed his daughter to hang on to his arm, but when she attempted to pull him away from the sink he resisted. 'Right now, your mother and I have some things to say to one another. Why don't you go upstairs and watch television? I promise I won't leave without saying goodbye.'

'Goodbye!' Daisy looked disappointed now. 'You're not really going, are you?'

'We'll see,' said Ben evenly, tucking a strand of hair behind her ear. His own hair was almost as long as Daisy's, Rachel noticed scornfully. Ben had really got into the artist's mould. She was surprised he wasn't wearing an earring.

Daisy hunched her shoulders. 'I'm not allowed to watch television,' she said sulkily, and Ben looked to Rachel for an explanation.

'I—yes, you can,' she muttered quickly, not wanting to get into another discussion concerning Daisy's discipline. 'Do as your father says, darling. We'll forget all about Mr Caldwell this time.'

'Caldwell?' Ben arched an interrogative brow as Daisy trudged reluctantly out of the room, and Rachel waited until she heard the little girl going upstairs, before she answered briefly.

'A little upset at work, that's all. It wasn't important. Now——' She squared her shoulders. 'What did you come here for? I told you the gist of what there was to tell this morning. The fact that I want a divorce shouldn't really surprise you.'

'Did I say it did?' Ben straightened away from the sink. 'But I don't think this is the place to be having this discussion,' he went on neutrally. 'Why don't we go into the other room?' His brow arched. 'Unless it's already occupied, of course.'

'Already occupied?' Rachel looked at him blankly for a moment before comprehension dawned. 'Oh—no. Simon's not here right now,' she assured him coolly. 'We can go in there if you like. Though I can't imagine what we have to talk about.'

'Can't you?' Ben shrugged. Then, 'Simon,' he remarked experimentally. 'Simon what?'

'Does it matter?' Rachel endeavoured not to sound as resentful as she felt as she led the way into the family-room. She saw her empty wine glass on the mantelpiece and wished she'd carried it into the kitchen with her. 'Who he is needn't concern you.'

'Like hell!' For the first time, Ben exhibited some emotion other than the guarded hostility he had revealed so briefly on his arrival, and Rachel felt an unexpected twinge of fear. 'Do you honestly think you can just tell me you want to marry someone else, without any reaction from me?'

Rachel swallowed. She had been going to sit down in one of the velvet armchairs beside the fire, but his vehemence—his violence—kept her nervously on her feet. 'I didn't think you'd care,' she replied carefully, linking her fingers together at her waist. 'Um—why don't you sit down?'

Ben had halted just inside the door of the room, and was presently looking about him, evidently registering the changes that had been made since he was last here. There was no particular expression on his dark face as his brooding gaze slid over the silk-printed curtains at the windows and alighted on the set of ceramic tiles that had taken the place of the original water-colour that used to hang above the fireplace. But she knew he was remembering how they had chosen the furnishings for this room together. It was their first attempt at interior designing, and she recalled how proud they had been of their efforts. Which was why she had torn down the curtains and stowed the picture away in the loft when he left, she remembered tensely. She hadn't been able to afford to totally redecorate the house, but in her own small way she had effected a modest transformation.

Now, Ben moved further into the room, and, desperate for something to do, Rachel went to draw the curtains. How many times in the past couple of years had she drawn these curtains, she reflected, wondering where Ben was and who he was with? Well, tonight she knew, but, conversely, it gave her no relief.

'I will have a drink,' Ben remarked, behind her, and she swung round, half guiltily, to find him opening the doors of the bureau. In the old days they had always kept a supply of wines and spirits in the cupboard below the bookcase, but no longer. He straightened, frowning. 'Where is it?'

'Where's what?' asked Rachel innocently, and had the satisfaction of seeing his frustration for a change.

'The Scotch,' he replied sardonically. 'Don't tell me: you keep it in the sitting-room these days. Another attempt to alter the old order, Rachel? I noticed you'd moved the picture. Where is it? Under your bed, with pins stuck in it?'

'Why would I do that?' Rachel was proud of her control. 'It wasn't a picture of you.'

His smile was sardonic. 'Point taken,' he conceded drily. 'Now—where the hell is that Scotch? You may not need one, but I surely do.'

Rachel pressed her lips together for a moment, and then gave in. 'If you must know, it's in the kitchen,' she told him resignedly. 'In the cupboard above the fridge. I don't keep much alcohol in the house, as it happens. I don't like spirits, and in any case it's too expensive.'

Ben let that go without comment, leaving the room briefly to get the whisky, before coming back again, bottle and glass in hand. He poured himself a generous measure, then, raising the glass to his lips, he offered her a silent toast, savouring the single malt with evident appreciation.

Rachel watched him half apprehensively. She was fighting the urge to demand that he state what he'd come for and go, and only the fact that she might inadvertently reveal how nervous he made her was keeping her silent.

Besides, she chided herself again, what was she worried about? It wasn't as if she was afraid of him. At no time had Ben ever threatened her or her custody of Daisy.

'So——' Ben's eyes flickered over her stiff erect figure, 'you're looking well.'

'Thank you.' Rachel refrained from returning the compliment, even if it was true. Ben did look well; a little leaner than she remembered, but disgustingly healthy none the less. He evidently didn't spend all his time labouring over a hot typewriter or a word processor or whatever it was he used to write his books these days. His body was taut, not to say hard, and she guessed he must still work out once or twice a week. Unless his romantic exploits constituted a viable alternative...

'You've put on some weight,' he added, lowering his glass and surveying her rounded hips with a critical eye. 'But it suits you,' he added. 'I always did think you were too thin.'

'And your opinion is the only one that matters, I suppose?' flashed Rachel angrily, immediately feeling as fat as a couch potato. 'Honestly, Ben, your arrogance is amazing! Believe it or not, but I don't give a—a——'

'Damn?' he supplied pleasantly, but she ignored him.

'A monkey's,' she asserted, with some relish, hoping he got the hidden message, 'what you think I look like.'

'You used to,' he reminded her, the expression in those dark eyes hidden by the narrowing of his lashes. 'So, why don't you tell me about this new man in your life? I imagine you care what he thinks.'

'Yes, I do.' Wishing he would sit down so that she could do the same, Rachel steeled her knees against their embarrassing tendency to shake. 'He—he's everything you're not: sweet, and kind—and *faithful*.'

Ben didn't look impressed. 'He sounds like a blood-hound,' he remarked unkindly, and Rachel felt like slapping his mocking face. 'Does Daisy share your views?'

Rachel drew a deep breath. 'Daisy—Daisy doesn't know Simon as well as I do.'

'What's that supposed to mean?'

'It means what it says.' Rachel couldn't sustain his cool interrogative stare any longer without betraying that she wasn't at all convinced what Daisy's feelings were. Turning away, she pretended to adjust a fold in one of the curtains, before continuing carefully, 'Daisy doesn't know Simon that well yet.'

'No?'

'No.'

'But she likes him?'

Behind her, Ben's voice was disturbingly persistent, and Rachel had to turn round again without having gained any advantage from the brief reprieve. 'I—I haven't discussed it with her,' she replied, not altogether truthfully. 'Um—naturally, she's very loyal——'

'To me?'

'To our marriage,' Rachel amended firmly. 'She is only eight, Ben. Obviously she still hopes there's some chance of us—of our——'

'—getting back together?'

'Absurd, isn't it?' Rachel managed to sound suitably amused at the suggestion. 'I've told her how it is. She just doesn't——'

'How is it?'

His question disconcerted her—as it was meant to do, she realised impatiently. He had emptied his glass now, and was waiting for her answer with what she could only identify as mild derision in his expression. The fact that he was baiting her gave her a feeling of frustration, and it was doubly infuriating to know that he could still do it so easily.

'Can we keep to the point, Ben?' she enquired, trying to ignore the heat that was invading her face once again at his words. 'I'm not enjoying this, even if you are, and I'd appreciate it if——'

'I thought that was the point,' he interrupted her obliquely, cradling his empty glass between his palms. 'I'd like to know what you've told her. Am I still the evil seducer of pubescent women?'

'I never told her th——' Rachel broke off abruptly, realising he was only trying to provoke her into defending herself once more. 'You know perfectly well that so far as Daisy is concerned, you're her hero.' Her lips twisted with conscious irony. 'But then, heroes are in short supply these days, and she doesn't have a lot of experience.'

'Unlike her mother?' suggested Ben, putting down his glass, and pushing his hand into the pockets of his trousers, and Rachel drew in a steadying breath.

His action had made her unwillingly aware of how lovingly the fabric of his trousers followed the muscles of his hips and thighs. Though she didn't want to notice it, the fine wool delineated the strength and leanness of his bones, accentuating the power in his legs and moulding the swell of his sex. She had forgotten how physical he was, she realised. Forgotten what it was like to be aware of a man in any way other than an intellectual one. With Simon, it was his kindness and his personality that had drawn her to him first; his ability to treat her like someone important, someone special. She'd deliberately obliterated the sexual attraction Ben had always had for her, and it was disturbing to realise that it had not been erased, only buried beneath a layer of pain and bitterness.

But it was only a *physical* attraction, she admonished herself grimly. The kind of attraction a rabbit might have for a snake.

'I said—unlike her mother?' Ben reminded her softly, and Rachel was suddenly aware of how long she had been standing there staring at him.

'I—no,' she answered hurriedly, wrapping her arms across her midriff in unknowing protection. 'Not at all.' She cleared her throat and her voice strengthened. 'I don't know any heroes, I'm afraid.'

'Not even Simon?' he prodded gently, and she forced herself to meet his mocking gaze without flinching.

'I'm not a child, Ben,' she told him coolly. 'I don't need a hero to satisfy my fantasies. An ordinary man will do very well. Someone who doesn't need constant reassurance that he's still got what it takes to—how would you put it?—to pull the birds?'

CHAPTER FOUR

BEN'S mouth compressed. 'Still the same old argument,' he remarked without rancour. 'I thought you'd at least attempt to convince me you'd fallen madly in love with this guy, whoever he is.'

Rachel caught her breath. 'I do love Simon,' she exclaimed hotly, but Ben only lifted his shoulders in a careless shrug.

'You're not—*in love* with him, though, are you?' he commented smoothly. 'There is a distinction.'

'Falling in love is for teenagers, Ben,' Rachel retorted, despising herself for even arguing with him over something so futile. 'Simon and I are adults. We know what it takes to make a relationship work. It takes patience, and commitment, and a willingness to share one another's problems. We're going to work together to provide a stable environment for Daisy to grow up in.'

'My God!' Ben gazed at her disbelievingly for a moment, and then flung himself down on to the sofa. With his arms draped along the back and his leg hooked comfortably over one of the arms, he looked up at her with wry amusement. 'Where's your soapbox, Rachel? When did you get to be such a prig?'

Rachel started for the door. 'If you've just come here to insult me——' she began, but she never got to finish her sentence. As she brushed past the sofa, Ben leaned forward and caught her arm, and his husky, 'I didn't,' drove all coherent protest from her head. For a heart-stopping moment, all she could think of was the cool strength in the fingers that were linked about her wrist, and that although she had wanted him to sit down earlier she had never intended he should make himself so completely at home.

47

But the familiarity of his actions arrested the wild sweetness flowering inside her. Dear God, she thought incredulously, had he only to touch her for her to fall apart? Just because she still possessed some lingering mind-set that reacted automatically to certain stimulants was no reason to give him any leeway. He knew what he was doing. He always had. And she mustn't ever forget it.

So now she said, with as much resignation in her voice as she could muster, 'Let go of me, Ben. This isn't going to work.'

He didn't let her go, of course. He just sat there, smoothing his thumb over the fine web of veins on the inner side of her wrist, looking up at her with dark questing eyes. And, conversely, though she had thought that having him in that position would give her the advantage, it didn't.

'What isn't going to work?' he asked, and there was no mockery in his tone now. 'Aren't I allowed to touch you? You used to like me to do a lot more than this.'

'Ben!' She spoke his name through clenched teeth. 'Will you stop behaving as if your being here had any more meaning than a peevish desire to thwart me? You don't care what I do. You haven't cared what I did for the past eighteen months. You just don't like the idea that someone else can make me happy!'

He looked down then, and she thought briefly that she had achieved her objective. But, instead of releasing her, he bent his head and let his tongue touch her skin, shocking her intensely, and sending little tongues of fire shooting up her arm. 'Of course I care about you,' he said roughly. 'Whatever you believe, I always have.'

She jerked away from him then, snatching her arm out of his grasp and cradling it against her, as if the pain she'd felt was physical. But she could feel only anger inside her, anger and frustration, and ridiculously, though she fought them off, the anguished sting of tears behind her eyes.

'Don't you ever——?' she was beginning hoarsely, when once again she didn't get to finish her sentence. The sound of footsteps on the stairs forced her to break off what she was saying, and Daisy's voice drifted plaintively from the safety of the lower landing,

'Can I come down now?' she called, and although Rachel wanted to deter her, Ben was quick to seize the advantage.

'Yes, come on down, sweetheart,' he shouted, holding his wife's resentful gaze as he got up from the sofa. 'We're in here. Having a cosy chat.'

Rachel was up at dawn. She hadn't slept much at all, and she was relieved when the birds signalled it was time to get up. Well, maybe not for everyone, she conceded, filling the kettle at the sink. But at least she didn't feel she was so out of the ordinary being downstairs at this time. The milkman was about, and the postman, and she had no doubt Simon was up, too, preparing his dairy herd for milking.

Thinking of Simon brought an uneasy catch to her throat. If she'd even thought Ben might turn up on her doorstep last night, she'd have made sure Simon was present. She'd known it would be awkward, telling Ben about her plans, but she'd never expected to have to do so face to face. As it was, she was left with the uneasy knowledge that nothing had been decided at all. Daisy's presence—and Ben's refusal to discuss anything in front of her—had negated any agreement. She was no nearer knowing now how Ben felt about it than she was before he swept back into her life.

Well, hardly swept back, she amended, frowning as she spooned tea into the pot. It was a figure of speech, born out of the way his headlights had swept the room the night before. But it fitted the facts. He had invaded her territory once again.

She sighed. That was why she was up at the crack of dawn, wondering what today was going to bring. After last night's little fiasco, she now had to tell Simon that she'd made no progress towards rationalising the situation whatsoever. She also had to tell him that Ben had come to the house, and that if Daisy had had her way, he would have spent the night in the guest-room.

But at least Ben had drawn the line there. Whether for Rachel's benefit—which she doubted—or for some nefarious reason of his own, he had declined his daughter's attempts to keep them together. He'd booked a room at the Old Swan, he'd told her ruefully, and he couldn't let the landlord down. As if he'd get the chance, Rachel had brooded indignantly. This was still her home, even if he did hold a controlling interest.

The kettle boiled, and she made the tea, carrying the pot and the cup into the snug, which was one room Ben hadn't entered the previous evening. They'd used to use it as a games-room in the old days. There were board games, and a television and video recorder, and a stack of video films, both pre-recorded and home-made. They had kept a record of Daisy's development on video film in those early days, and her first attempts to walk and talk were captured for posterity. Rachel didn't know if Ben ever videoed Daisy these days. If he did, she hadn't heard about it, but that was no guarantee that he didn't.

Now, Rachel seated herself in the squashy leather chair beneath the window, and tucked her legs beneath the folds of her old velvet dressing gown. Then, sipping her tea, she stared rather despairingly into space. What was she going to do? She had to get an answer from Ben, but how was she going to handle it?

It had seemed almost easy yesterday, ringing him and asking for a divorce. She hadn't looked forward to doing it. No one would. But it was more than eighteen months since they'd had any contact, other than through Daisy, and she'd assumed he'd jump at the chance to be given his freedom.

Or had she?

Hadn't she had some qualms about how he'd take it? Hadn't she worried a little as to what his reaction would be about Daisy moving home and moving school? But nothing had prepared her for Ben's turning up on her doorstep. Nothing had prepared her for the way he'd acted. The memory of how he'd held her and kissed her hard caused a wave of anger and revulsion to wash over her. How dared he behave as if he still had the right to touch her? How dared he mouth words of affection which were blatantly so false?

No wonder the evening had been such an absolute disaster. After what had happened, Rachel had been in no state to talk rationally about anything. Instead, she had been the unwilling third at Ben and Daisy's reunion, speaking only when spoken to, and contributing little to the conversation.

Which was surely an indication of her own weakness, she reflected irritably. Ben and Daisy had done what they liked, and she had said nothing to stop them. She could tell herself that if Simon's name had been mentioned she'd have made a stand, but would she? Hadn't Ben successfully neutralised her opposition so that he could take control?

And how had he done it? she asked herself bitterly. By taking hold of her arm and touching her skin with his tongue. She shivered, as the remembrance brought another wave of apprehension. Why had he done it? And more importantly, why had she cared?

Her cup was empty and, glad of the activity, she got up to refill it. Outside the window, a pale beam of sunlight caught in the wing mirror of the car that was still parked on her drive and flashed it back at her in a shaft of brilliance. *Ben's* car, she acknowledged frustratedly, parked outside *her* house all night. It was to be hoped that Simon would believe her when she told him Ben had not stayed there as well. And she intended to tell him, before someone else chose to make the connection.

All the same, the sight of the sleek Mercedes was just another cause for her resentment. Ben had nothing to lose here, while she had everything. She wanted her relationship with Simon to work. She wanted the security he could give. Whatever Ben said, she had to make her own choices. If she didn't, she'd be forever in his shadow.

Daisy came clattering down the stairs soon after seven o'clock. She wasn't usually up so early, but her mother guessed she was excited because her father was staying in the village. Last night, in an effort to avoid another argument with her daughter, Rachel had agreed that the child could miss school today. Ben was coming to collect her before Rachel left for work, and although it wasn't the wisest decision she had ever made, Rachel had had little choice in the matter.

Evidently Daisy had investigated her mother's bedroom before she came downstairs and found it empty, because she came looking for her straight away. 'What are you doing in here?' she exclaimed, and Rachel noticed with a pang that the little girl was already dressed. How long did it usually take her to get Daisy to put her clothes on on a school morning? she wondered wryly. Longer than it took her to dress in her best pink tracksuit anyway, she conceded, aware of who it was who had bought the expensive outfit in the first place. It suited her, there was no question about that. But Rachel was not in the mood to appreciate it this morning, particularly with the prospect of another difficult day ahead of her.

'I'm drinking my tea,' she replied now, finishing her second cup with a flourish and getting up from the chair again. 'What do you think?'

'But why are you sitting in here?' asked Daisy curiously. 'You usually have your morning tea in the kitchen.'

'I felt like it,' responded Rachel, doing her best not to sound peevish. 'What do you want for breakfast? Cereal or an egg?'

'Actually, Daddy said he'd take me out for breakfast,' offered Daisy, colouring a little. 'I mean, you'll be leaving for the shop soon, and he said it would save you having to do it.'

'I do it every other morning,' retorted Rachel, picking up her cup and marching aggressively into the kitchen. 'I suppose this was all arranged when you saw him off last night. What else did you say when I wasn't there? Did you tell him you'd soon be moving to Kingsmead?'

It was an unfair question and Rachel knew it, but she had no one else to expunge her ire on and Daisy was there.

Daisy followed her into the kitchen, pausing beside one of the kitchen chairs, and scuffing her heel on its rung. 'No,' she said, now, somewhat sulkily. 'We didn't talk about Mr Barrass at all. You know we didn't. You were there. Why didn't you tell him yourself if you wanted him to know?'

'Well, of course I wanted him to know,' exclaimed Rachel, stung into a reply. She submerged the contrition she had been feeling beneath a swell of indignation. 'I didn't get the chance, that's all.'

Daisy's lower lip jutted. 'You could have told him,' she muttered. 'While I was in my room. What did you talk about while I was upstairs anyway? You looked sort of flustered when I came down.'

Rachel was glad she had her back to her daughter when Daisy made this remark. The girl could be quite astute at times, and it wouldn't do for her to start hoping that her mother was not as determined on her course of action as she'd thought. 'I was annoyed, that's all,' she said, which was certainly true. 'Your father had no right to come here uninvited.'

'I thought you did invite him.' Daisy regarded her mother suspiciously now. 'Daddy said you phoned him yesterday morning.'

'Not to invite him here,' Rachel insisted shortly, reaching for a tea-towel to dry her cup. 'As you are well aware, I needed to talk to him about—about——'

'—Mr Barrass,' supplied Daisy gloomily and Rachel sighed.

'About Simon, yes,' she agreed, choosing the least controversial of the alternatives. So far, she had avoided mentioning the divorce to Daisy. But she was sure the child must know.

All the same...

'You didn't, though, did you?' Daisy pointed out. 'You just talked about my school and the shop.' She grimaced. 'When you talked at all.'

'I think you have far too much to say for yourself,' returned Rachel crisply, and then chided herself anew as Daisy's face dropped. If she wasn't careful, she was going to alienate the child completely, and all because she was letting Ben's arrogance get under her skin.

'Well, at least Daddy likes to hear my opinion about things,' Daisy retorted now, but there was a faint tremor in her voice that was unmistakable. However confidently she acted sometimes, she was really frightened and uncertain. Not sure of what was expected of her, and anxious about the future.

And, at once, Rachel relented. 'I like to hear your opinions, too, darling,' she exclaimed, laying down the tea-towel, and crossing the room to where Daisy was standing. With a rueful smile, she gathered the little girl into her arms and gave her a swift hug. 'I'm sorry if I was grumpy. Your father has that effect on me.'

Daisy sniffed, returning the hug for a moment before drawing back. 'Why does Daddy make you grumpy? He didn't used to.'

'No—well——' That was one topic Rachel didn't want to get into. It had been hard enough at the time, explaining why Elena had left at the same time as her father. Later, she supposed, the child would demand a proper explanation. But, for the present, Rachel would prefer to avoid the issue. 'We're just not—compatible,' she offered now, and saw her daughter's face cloud over again. 'But we are still—friends,' she appended, revising that to 'still speaking to one another' in her own mind,

'Then why does Daddy make you grumpy?' argued Daisy, returning to her original question, and Rachel thought how wonderful it must be to see things so simply.

'Well—because he does,' she replied, smoothing the little girl's dark hair behind her ears, and regarding her with some regret. 'It happens sometimes, darling. People think they're happy together, but then they discover they're not.'

Daisy frowned. 'Was it my fault?' she asked, voicing a doubt that had evidently been troubling her, and Rachel tugged her close again.

'Of course not!' she exclaimed. 'You're the best thing that ever happened to us.' She kissed the top of her daughter's head. 'I think you'll find that's one thing on which your father and I can agree.'

And it was while she was standing, cradling the child to her, that Rachel looked up and found Ben watching them through the kitchen window. How long he had been there, she had no idea, but she was relieved that he couldn't possibly have heard what they were saying. Nevertheless, the idea that he should be creeping about her garden at this early hour infuriated her. How dared he behave as if he had a right to be there? Why couldn't he have come to the front door and rung the bell like anyone else?

Because he wasn't like anyone else, she thought, her mind automatically supplying the answer, as her emotions reacted unnervingly to his presence. Meeting his eyes, glimpsing the satisfaction in their depths, she felt an overwhelming feeling of inadequacy. Ben had always had that effect on her, and time—and changing circumstances—hadn't altered it one whit. Her heart lurched. In jeans and a navy blue sweatshirt, he was disturbingly attractive, and she couldn't help comparing his lean muscularity to Simon's solid appearance. But that was the difference between them, she reminded herself angrily, putting the child away from her and reaching for the handle of the door. Simon was solid, and dependable, two characteristics that Ben was sadly without.

'What are you doing, skulking about out there?' she demanded, using her anger as a means of defence, and Ben came to rest indolently against the doorframe.

'I wasn't skulking about,' he replied mildly, smiling as Daisy showed her excitement at his appearance by flinging herself upon him. 'I remembered we always used to have breakfast in the kitchen, and I didn't want to startle you.'

'Well, you did,' retorted Rachel shortly, suddenly aware that in her old dressing-gown and fluffy slippers, her tawny hair a tangled mess about her shoulders, she didn't look anything like the controlled being she'd intended to present to him.

'Are you taking me to the hotel for breakfast?' Daisy demanded eagerly, and her father pulled a thoughtful face.

'If you like,' he said. 'Or perhaps your mother would like to invite me to have breakfast here. She used to be a mean hand with crispy bacon and scrambled eggs.'

'I don't eat breakfast any more,' Rachel responded, not altogether truthfully. She seldom left the house without eating at least one slice of toast and marmalade, but this morning she didn't feel as if she could eat a thing. Once again, Ben was giving her the runaround, and she was doing nothing to stop him.

'I'd rather go to the hotel,' Daisy intervened, much to her mother's relief, not at all enthusiastic about eating breakfast at home, even if her father was. 'Do they serve pancakes at the Old Swan, like Mrs Cornwell makes?'She turned to her mother. 'Oh, Mum, you should taste Mrs Cornwell's pancakes. They're really delicious!'

'Possibly,' Ben was beginning, while Rachel absorbed the fact that there were things her daughter and her father had shared about which she knew nothing. At least she knew who Mrs Cornwell was, she reflected gratefully. Not one of Ben's dolly-birds, but the housekeeper he had employed after several unsuccessful months of coping for himself.

'Then can we go?' Daisy persisted, evidently half afraid her mother was going to change her mind. 'I'm all ready, and I'm really hungry.'

'Well——' Ben began again, but this time Rachel took the initiative.

'In a minute, darling,' she said, earning a frustrated look from her daughter but ignoring it. 'I'd like to have a quick word with your father.' She paused, then said, albeit a little acidly, 'If he has the time.'

Ben straightened, and came into the kitchen, closing the door behind him. 'Are you sure you don't want to make me breakfast?' he asked, leaning back against the glass panels and folding his arms. 'Just for old times' sake, of course.'

'In your dreams,' retorted Rachel, wrapping the folds of her dressing-gown closer about her. 'Go upstairs for a few minutes, will you, Daisy? This won't take long.'

'Again?'

Daisy's reaction was resentful, and Rachel controlled her own temper with difficulty. 'A few minutes, Daisy,' she said, giving the little girl a warning look. 'You don't want me to forbid you from having breakfast with your father, do you?'

'You couldn't, anyway,' declared Daisy defiantly, but this time Ben took a hand.

'She could,' he said, giving her a gentle push towards the hall. 'Do as you're told, baby. As your mother says, this won't take long.'

Daisy went, albeit with many a wounded backward glance, but Rachel had more important things on her mind. 'I can discipline my own daughter,' she said, first of all, returning to her previous position by the sink.

Then, when Ben made no comment, she added rather ungraciously, 'Do you want to sit down?'

'Why?' Ben was sardonic. 'Do you think what you're going to say is going to shock me?'

'It may.' Rachel refused to be disconcerted. 'Simon wants Daisy and me to live with him at Kingsmead, while we're waiting for the divorce.'

CHAPTER FIVE

THERE was silence for a pregnant moment, and then Ben straightened away from the door. 'What was it you said earlier?' he asked, and briefly the mildness of his tone deceived her into thinking he had taken her news calmly. 'In your dreams?' he suggested, immediately dispelling her moment of relief. 'This is Daisy's home, Rachel. For as long as you remain my wife.'

Rachel's face suffused with colour. 'Which won't be for much longer,' she countered, stung into an uncontrolled response. 'What a hypocrite you are, Ben. You live your life exactly how and where you choose, but just because I want to make some changes in my life you suddenly decide to play the heavy husband!'

'It's not a role I'd have chosen, believe me,' he retorted, lowering his hands to his sides and pushing himself away from the door. 'And as Daisy's mother, I'd have thought, you'd understand the position. Or does sleeping with your lover count for more than considering your daughter's feelings?'

Rachel caught her breath. 'How—how dare you?'

'How dare I what?' Ben had taken another step towards her, and, while he wasn't making a frontal attack, his approach was just as menacing. 'What did you think I'd say? Oh, yeah—go ahead; disrupt Daisy's life for as long as it takes for you to come to your senses?'

'To come to my senses?' Rachel's back was to the sink, and now she placed one hand on the unit at either side of her. The action pushed the lapels of her dressing gown forward and exposed the rounded neckline of the T-shirt she used to sleep in, but she couldn't help that. It wasn't as if she was revealing anything, and the attitude—she hoped—was one of defiance. 'Exactly what am I supposed to come to my senses over? I've told you: Simon and I love one another. And—and he'll make a good father for Daisy. As you can see, she needs a man's influence.'

'I agree.' Ben took another step towards her. 'Mine. She needs my influence. I'm her father, Rachel, not Simple Simon, whoever he may be. And if you think I'm going to hand my daughter over to some country bumpkin you're mistaken. If you want to change the rules, OK, but if you do, Daisy comes to live with me!'

Rachel's breathing felt constricted. 'You're not serious!' she exclaimed, pressing her spine back against the unit behind her. 'Besides——' she had to say something or her panic would overwhelm her '—you agreed that I should have custody. You can't take her away. The courts wouldn't let you?'

'Try me,' said Ben softly, lifting one hand and stroking the line of her jaw. 'You didn't really think I'd make it that easy? Oh, love, you're talking to the wrong man!'

'Don't touch me!' Rachel jerked her face away from his caressing hand, but all she achieved was for Ben to mimic her action by putting a hand at either side of her, imprisoning her against the sink like a butterfly on a pin. 'And—I'm not your love,' she added, for good measure. 'You won't get away with this, Ben. I've got weapons, too.'

'Weapons!' He echoed the threat with mocking indulgence, in no way alarmed by her puny attempt to defend herself. 'Oh, Rachel, how did we ever come to this?'

'If you don't let me go——'

'If I don't let you go—what?' His eyes were on her mouth, and although she knew it was crazy she found herself pressing her lips together, as if by doing so she could prevent the sensuous brush of that dark, disturbing gaze. 'What will you do?' he taunted. 'Scream?' He shook his head. 'Oh, no, I don't think you'll do that,

Rachel. We don't want to upset Daisy when it's not necessary.'

'She won't be upset if you'll just accept that other people are entitled to a life as well as you,' retorted Rachel breathlessly. 'It's not as if she's your only child, is she? What happened to Elena's baby, or aren't I allowed to ask?'

'I haven't the faintest idea what happened to Elena's baby,' he retorted carelessly. 'I don't even know where she is. She went back to France, I imagine. It's no concern of mine.'

'How can you say that?' She lifted her hand and pushed back the tumbled weight of her hair. 'Ben, this is childish. Whatever do you expect to achieve?'

'You didn't cut your hair.' His response was oblique, and Rachel raised her eyes to the ceiling, as if seeking divine intervention. But the truth was, his nearness still unnerved her. She despised him, but she couldn't ignore him, and the strain of the situation was getting to her.

'What do you want?' she tried again, wondering if by reasoning with him she might be any more successful. God, if only Simon were here, she thought despairingly, latching on to the image of her fiancé in a vain attempt to avoid Ben's raw reality. If he were here, this wouldn't be happening. If he knew what Ben was doing, he'd stop him in his tracks.

'You.'

Ben's response almost went unnoticed as Rachel struggled with her feelings. She was so busy trying to find a way to escape him that his words scarcely registered in her brain. But then, as he bent his head towards her, as he caught the tender lobe of her ear between his teeth and bit the soft skin, she understood, and the meaning of his answer caused the blood to pound hotly through her veins.

'You're crazy,' she said, but her hopes of handling the situation rationally were rapidly receding. Her attempts to appear indifferent to his advances were not going to do it, and, taking a deep breath, she pressed both hands firmly against his chest.

The sensual heat of his skin striking up through the material of his sweatshirt was almost her undoing. It reminded her so much of other occasions, when touching him had not been such a traumatic experience. His body had always been so hard and smooth, so leanly muscled, that it had been a pleasure to slide her hands across his chest and midriff, and the flat contours of his stomach. He didn't have a hairy body—unlike Simon, she admitted, guilty at the direction of her thoughts—but the fine hair that arrowed down to his navel was essentially masculine, curly and virile, and amazing soft. Thicker, too, where it reached the heated junction of his thighs...

'Am I?'

Rachel came to with an effort, realising that, while she had been allowing her thoughts to drift, Ben had moved in closer. Her resistance had waned at the reckless slant her thoughts had taken, and she was vulnerable now as she hadn't been before. He was nuzzling her neck with his lips, finding the erratic pulse at her jawline, and measuring its beating with his tongue. If she turned her head a fraction, he was going to find her mouth, and the dangers of that happening were too awful to consider.

How had she got herself into this position? she wondered incredulously, as the hard strength of his leg pushed against the clamped tightness of her thighs. How had she let him get this close, when all he really wanted was to humiliate her? Well, whatever his intentions, he wasn't going to get away with it—however weak her knees felt when she looked at the thin-lipped arrogance of his mouth...

'You don't want me,' she insisted, making her neck ache with the effort to get away from him. 'You just want to control me, to destroy any chance I might have of finding happiness with someone else.' Her voice had risen as she spoke, and she could hear the thread of panic running through it. 'You don't really care if I marry

Simon. You just can't stand the thought that he can do what you never could!'

'Never?'

Ben's tone had hardened now, and she guessed it hadn't been the wisest of moves, making him angry while he had her in his grasp. With a hostile expellation of his breath he caught her chin between his fingers and forced her face up to his. Then, while she was still reeling from the shock, he ground his mouth down on hers, crushing her lips against her teeth.

'Never?' he said again, against her mouth, the moist heat of his breathing invading her nostrils and forcing her to open her mouth so that she could get some air. And when she did so, his tongue slid wetly between her lips, almost suffocating her with its hungry possession.

Rachel's senses swam. For a mindless moment, she couldn't think; couldn't breathe; couldn't even react, though her senses were working overtime. The taste of him, the feel of him, as he pressed her back against the sink, was all she was really aware of. It wasn't pleasurable, it wasn't desirable, but her limbs ached with a hunger she hadn't felt for years. Hard and fierce, Ben's mouth sought and ravaged her sweetness, and although in some far distant corner of her brain she knew she should be resisting this, the needs he was inspiring were impossible to ignore.

She felt his arousal almost instinctively. The bones of his thighs and hips and pelvis were all impaling her against the wood behind her, but it was the swelling hardness between his legs that caused the sudden awareness. His maleness thrust against her, straining the fabric of his jeans and unerringly finding the joining of her legs, where her own unwanted response was pulsing slickly between her thighs.

Dear God, she thought, she wanted him. Not gently or intelligently, as she wanted Simon, but hotly and hungrily, with a passion that was wholly sexual. And, as he drove his fingers into her hair and brought her mouth more fully to his, she knew that she had only to go on like this and he'd be lifting the hem of her nightshirt, and loosening his zip.

It wouldn't be the first time that had happened. In the early days of their marriage, before the miscarriages she had had after Daisy was born had turned making love into a frightening gamble, they had loved one another whenever and wherever they liked. Sharing their bodies—sharing their *love*—had seemed the most natural thing in the world, and Rachel would never have believed in those days that anything—or anyone—could come between them.

But something had—*someone* had—and just because she was suffering some kind of mid-life crisis there was no reason to forget what Ben had done. He was just tormenting her now, attempting to prove to her—and to himself—that if he wanted her, he could have her.

For the past few months he had kept his distance, probably due to the knowledge that what he had done had spoiled her for other men. And in the early days after their separation she had been too numb to even think of going out with anyone else, and Daisy must have kept him informed of her lack of interest in his sex.

Besides, if their behaviour before they split up was anything to go by, Ben must have thought there was no danger of her ever getting involved with anyone else. After her last miscarriage, her fear of getting pregnant had destroyed the spontaneity of their love-making, and she couldn't remember the last time she had felt so recklessly alive.

But that was no excuse for what she was doing—for what *he* was doing. Just because her legs were shaking and her knees were trembling, and the urgency of his mouth was turning all her bones to water, it was no reason to allow him to get away with this. Simon made her tremble—or he would if she let him get this close to her. Simon was the man she was going to marry. Ben was just seeing how far she'd let him go...

But, in the event, it was the sound of Daisy coming down the stairs again that brought an end to her trial of fire. As Ben uttered a muffled oath and released her, she tried to tell herself that even without Daisy's intervention she would have put an end to it. But as she wrapped the folds of her dressing-gown more closely about her and met his sardonic gaze she knew she'd never convince him of that. Well, not on today's showing anyway, she conceded, meeting his stare with cold contempt. But whether that contempt was for him or herself she couldn't be certain. All she knew was that he was a danger to her newfound happiness, and as unscrupulously selfish now as he'd ever been before.

By the time Daisy came along the passage however, Rachel had regained sufficient control over her emotions to be able to face her daughter without betraying her feelings. What had happened—what might be going to happen in the future—was not something she was prepared to deal with at this moment. She was going to get a divorce. Of that she had no doubt. And retain custody of Daisy, she asserted silently, whatever threats Ben might throw her way.

All the same, the tension in the room was palpable, and Daisy, for all her youth, was not indifferent to the atmosphere between her parents. 'Is something wrong?' she demanded, coming into the room wearing an expression that mingled impatience and anxiety in equal measures. 'I couldn't hear you talking. I was afraid you'd sent Daddy away.'

'Your mother wouldn't do that,' responded Ben drily, raking back his hair with a careless hand. His eyes flickered in Rachel's direction, and his lips twitched ever so slightly. 'Your mother was just reminding me of—old times.'

'Bastard!'

Behind the little girl's back, Rachel mouthed the word at him, but she wasn't even sure he saw her. Of course, if he had, he was unlikely to give her the satisfaction of acknowledging it. Propped on the edge of the table, he was totally in control.

'Well, can we go now?' exclaimed Daisy, somewhat fretfully, not really interested in what they had been doing so long as it didn't interfere with her outing. 'I've been waiting ages! Can't you talk to Mummy later?'

Like father, like daughter, thought Rachel peevishly, not at all surprised when Ben pushed himself away from the table and held out his hand to the little girl. 'Oh, yes,' he said, with a mocking smile, and Rachel knew he was daring her to make an issue of it, 'Mummy and I will have lots to talk about later. I'd better book my room at the Old Swan for a few days. We wouldn't want her to be disappointed.'

'Why can't you stay here?' protested Daisy at once, but evidently Ben had decided he had gone far enough for today.

'Come on, small fry,' he said, avoiding a direct answer. 'Our ham and eggs are waiting. And your mother's got to get ready for work. She doesn't want to be late, does she?'

Rachel managed to control herself until she heard the car pull away, but then she indulged herself in a veritable orgy of rude expletives. The pig, she thought, stamping up the stairs to her bedroom. How dared he imply she had any desire to see him or talk to him again? As far as he was concerned, it would have been infinitely wiser to leave all the negotiations to her solicitor. She should have known better than to try and reason with a conceited bastard like him.

Half an hour later, with the effects of a hot shower having pummelled most of her resentment out of her, Rachel stood before the mirror in her bedroom and tried to rationalise why she had been so furious in the first place. Ben had kissed her. He had held her and kissed her, and let her feel how easily he became aroused—but so what? It wasn't as if it had never happened before. They had been man and wife, for God's sake! Were still man and wife, in name at least. So why was she acting like an outraged virgin, just because Ben had behaved with a characteristic lack of principle?

Because she'd let him get away with it, a small voice jeered mockingly. She'd let him think, albeit inaccurately, that he could still get to her that way, and it infuriated her. She should have been on her guard. She should have known that his coming down here had not been to wish her well. He wanted her to question what she was doing. He wanted her off balance—and he had almost succeeded.

Which was why she felt so frustrated now, she thought, as she pulled off the towel she had wrapped around her hair when she came out of the shower. The silky mass tumbled in damp strands to her shoulders, but she barely noticed. All she knew, as she bent to plug in the drier, was that it got in the way. And she had no intention of getting it cut, after what Ben had said, she acknowledged irritably. Nothing he said or did was going to affect her in the slightest.

All the same, she found herself hesitating over which outfit she should wear for work. Her normal attire of a well-cut blouse and skirt—sometimes accompanied by a waistcoat or a sweater on colder days—suddenly seemed very formal, and it was only when she realised exactly why she was questioning her appearance that she hastily dressed in her usual clothes. She had no intention of trying to compete with the women Ben associated with in London. She was not svelte and she was not beautiful, and it would be foolish to pretend otherwise.

The phone rang as she was leaving the house, and although she was tempted to ignore it, the chance that it might be Mr Caldwell, ringing to ask her to collect some object before coming in to the shop, had her reaching reluctantly for the receiver.

'Yes?' she said, aware that her tone wasn't exactly friendly, but not altogether convinced that it mightn't be Ben, ringing to provoke her once again. However, the light, but rueful, voice that answered her was unmistakably feminine, and she found herself blinking in surprise.

'Mmm, you sound gloomy, darling,' the caller exclaimed mischievously. 'Did you get out of the wrong side of the bed this morning, or has that granddaughter of mine been doing something dreadful?'

'Mum!'

Rachel's astonishment was not feigned. It was three months since she had last spoken to her mother, just before she left for a prolonged visit with Rachel's brother in New Zealand. Rachel hadn't expected her back for another month, at least, and although it was good to hear from her, the timing wasn't exactly propitious.

'Yes, it's me,' Mrs Collins responded now, enjoying her daughter's consternation. 'The flight landed early, so I'm phoning you from the airport.'

'I see.' Rachel struggled to inject a note of enthusiasm into her voice. But it wasn't easy, with the problem of how to deal with Ben foremost in her mind, and she knew exactly what her mother would say when she told her what was going on.

'You don't sound exactly thrilled to hear from me,' Mrs Collins remarked now, her tone a little less lively than before, and Rachel hurried to reassure her.

'It's not that,' she said lamely, 'I mean, of course I'm pleased to hear from you, and I'm glad you're home safely. You should have let us know you were coming. I—might have been able to meet you at the airport.'

'Yes—well, it all happened rather suddenly,' replied her mother evasively. 'And it really doesn't matter now I'm here. And just in case you're interested, it was a very pleasant flight back. I slept for most of the latter half of the journey. I expect the jet-lag will hit me eventually, but right now, I feel wonderful.'

'That's good.' Rachel licked her lips. 'Well—I'm afraid you've caught me in a bit of a rush, that's all. I—I was late already, and now——'

'Now I'm holding you up. I know.' Her mother sounded understanding, and Rachel was relieved. 'But I did have a reason for calling. I thought I might come and spend a few days with you and Daisy before going back to my flat. What do you think about that?'

'Here?' Rachel knew she sounded dismayed, but she couldn't help it. That was all she needed right now: for her mother to arrive and find out what was going on. Mrs Collins didn't even know she and Simon were engaged, for heaven's sake. And, for all his faults, she had always had a soft spot for Ben.

'Where else?' her mother declared impatiently now. 'Rachel, is something wrong? Has that pig-farmer moved in with you or something, because if he has I should tell you, I don't think Daisy should——'

'No!' Rachel was indignant, and not giving her mother the chance to finish whatever piece of advice she had been about to offer, she went on grimly, 'And Simon is not a pig-farmer, as you very well know. He owns a very old and very beautiful dairy farm in the heart of the Gloucestershire countryside. And—and I'm proud to say he's asked me to marry him, as soon as Ben and I can get a divorce!'

She hadn't intended to blurt it out like that, and as soon as she had, she wished she hadn't. But her mother's sarcasm, coming on top of Ben's, had been just too much for her, and she waited with some apprehension for her mother's shocked reaction.

It wasn't long in coming. 'And does Ben know about this?'

Typically, Mrs Collins had leapt straight to the heart of the matter, and for a moment Rachel wondered if Ben hadn't been the reason her mother had cut short her holiday. But no. As far as she knew, he hadn't even known her mother was out of the country, and surely he wouldn't appeal to her own mother to intercede on his behalf.

Now, Rachel wished she had succumbed to the temptation not to answer the phone in the first place. This conversation wasn't getting any easier, and Cyril really didn't like his staff to be late.

'I've told him,' she offered now, wondering if there was any way she could avoid mentioning the fact that he was presently staying in the village. 'Look, Mum, I really must get going. You know what Mr Caldwell's like.'

'So, I'm not welcome at Wychwood at the moment?'

Mrs Collins sniffed, and Rachel realised there was no way she was going to get out of this. 'Of course you're welcome here,' she exclaimed, remembering how comparatively uncomplicated her life had seemed just a couple of days ago. 'But—well, I might as well tell you, Ben's here, too. He's come down to——' she crossed her fingers '—to discuss the arrangements for the divorce.'

'Ben's staying with you?' Her mother sounded positively delighted now, and Rachel wondered if she would have been so forgiving if he had been unfaithful to her. 'Oh, it'll be lovely to see him again.'

'He's staying at the Old Swan,' retorted Rachel dourly, in no mood to sing Ben's praises. 'I certainly didn't invite him here, but——' She broke off, realising she was in danger of revealing too much, and then continued curtly, 'He's come to see Daisy. I've—let her take a day off school. He's taken her for breakfast at the hotel.'

'I see.' Mrs Collins sounded as if she wasn't entirely convinced by her daughter's explanation, but the sound of the airport information system in the background had her hurrying to terminate the call. 'I've got to go,' she said. 'My luggage is coming through now, and I don't want to be last in line at Customs. I've checked with British Rail, and there's a train from Paddington at half-past ten. With a bit of luck, I should be in time to catch it. So, I'll see you at lunchtime probably. If not, I'll come to the shop and find you, hmm?'

'All right.'

Rachel's agreement was less than eager, but the prospect of another shortening of the odds against her was not something she could feel enthusiastic about. Ben had always been the blue-eyed boy—metaphorically speaking, of course, she amended, ignoring the shiver that feathered down her spine when she thought of his dark, disturbing gaze—so far as Mrs Collins was concerned. Even when Rachel had fled to London, after finding Elena and her husband together, her mother had warned her against jumping to the wrong conclusions. Even then, she had been trying to find excuses for him, and it was only when Rachel returned home and found Ben had already departed that Mrs Collins had had to accept that perhaps her daughter had been right.

Rachel put down the phone now, and stood staring at it for a moment. Dear God, what had she let herself in for now? With her mother here, it was going to be virtually impossible to have a serious conversation with her husband. And why, after spending so long abroad, was her mother so eager to come and stay with her daughter? Unless she'd had had some inkling of the situation, wouldn't she normally have wanted to go home?

CHAPTER SIX

RACHEL was in the stock-room when Cyril Caldwell came to find her. They had received a delivery of Danish porcelain that morning, and it was Rachel's job to unpack it, and categorise it for display. In consequence, her hands were dusty, and the news that she had a visitor caused another wave of harassment.

The conviction that it must be Ben brought two splashes of hot colour to her cheeks, and she wasn't amused when Mr Caldwell suggested she should look in a mirror before meeting her admirer.

'He's not my admirer,' retorted Rachel crossly, getting to her feet and smearing her dusty palms over her skirt. 'You know very well that he's my husband. And if you think that——'

'You and Barrass are married!'

Mr Caldwell looked staggered now, and Rachel stared at him blankly for a moment, before taking a hurried look through the curtain, that divided the two departments of the shop. Sure enough, Simon was standing stiffly beside the French *escritoire* Cyril had on display, and judging by his face he'd heard everything she'd said.

'Oh, sh-oot,' she muttered, barely audibly, before giving her boss a frustrated glance. Then, without giving a thought to her appearance, she swept purposefully through the curtain, ignoring Simon's scowling expression, as she pressed her lips to his cheek. 'What a lovely surprise!'

'Is it?'

Simon looked decidedly unconvinced, and she wondered with a pang what particular God she had offended to deserve this. 'Of course it is,' she exclaimed, allowing her hand to trail appealingly over his sleeve. 'I'm always

72

pleased to see you, Simon. I just didn't expect to see you this morning, that's all.'

'Why?' Simon wasn't in the mood to let her off the hook quite yet. 'Because you'd arranged to see your—*husband*?' The pause before the word, and the pointed way he said it, warned her he wasn't just angry because of what he had overheard. 'I understand Leeming spent last night in the village. Is it a coincidence that his car was parked outside your house all night?'

Rachel's hand fell to her side. So far this morning she had had to contend with a provocative soon-to-be-ex husband, a peevish mother, and a teasing employer. Dealing with Simon's unwarranted suspicions as well was not something she was prepared to tolerate, and although his feelings might be justified, surely she was owed some measure of trust? She refused to consider that her own behaviour had been less than responsible. What had happened between her and Ben had been at his initiation, not hers.

Now, she took a deep breath. 'Is that all you came for?' she asked, and she could tell by his sudden uncertainty that it was not the answer he had expected.

'Well, I——'

'Because if it is, I suggest it can wait until some other time.' Rachel's expression was as cold as his now. 'I have work to do, Simon. Mr Caldwell doesn't pay me to indulge in petty discussions about my private life!'

Simon was taken aback. 'I—don't consider this is a petty discussion, Rachel. It's obvious you were expecting him to come and see you here today. I understood—that is, you told me you were going to ring him, not invite him to visit you. How do you think I felt, when one of your neighbours informed me that his Mercedes was standing on your drive all night?'

Rachel expelled her breath. 'Mrs Reynolds.' The elderly woman who lived in the house opposite had nothing else to do all day but spy on the other occupants of the road.

'It doesn't matter who it was.' Simon was regaining his confidence. 'How would you feel if I'd invited my ex-wife to spend the night at Kingsmead?'

Rachel felt herself relaxing. 'You don't have an ex-wife, do you?' she asked, rather whimsically, as the humour of the situation overcame her indignation. But Simon didn't respond in kind.

'You know what I mean,' he declared testily, 'My mother was—*I* was—mortified.'

'Ah.' Rachel was beginning to understand. 'It was your mother who told you.' It didn't surprise her. Mrs Barrass had been the only woman in her son's life for far too long to surrender that role totally gracefully.

'It doesn't matter who told me,' Simon said again. 'The fact remains, it's true. Leeming is here, in Upper Morton, isn't he? But why is he here? What does he want? Didn't you tell him you wanted a divorce?'

'Of course I told him,' exclaimed Rachel shortly, casting a meaningful glance over her shoulder. She had no doubt that Cyril was listening to their exchange, and she had no wish for her affairs to be the source of any more gossip in the village.

It had been bad enough when Ben had left her, and she had been eternally grateful that Daisy's school was far enough away from Upper Morton for there to be no backlash there. But Daisy was older now. She couldn't be put off with prevarications any longer. And the last thing Rachel wanted was for her daughter to hear the story of their separation from anyone else but her.

'Look,' she said, when he still showed no inclination of taking the hint, 'I suggest we talk about this tonight. Pick me up about half-past seven. We can go and have a drink.'

Simon stiffened. 'Why can't I come to the house?' His lips curled. 'Or is your husband planning on staying indefinitely?'

'No.' Rachel silently seethed. 'Ben is not staying—well, not with me, anyway,' she amended. 'He's got a room at the Old Swan. Check on it, if you don't believe me. I'm sure Charlie Braddock will be glad to hear you're interested.'

Simon flushed. 'Then how can you leave Daisy?' he demanded. 'I thought Sandra was on holiday with her parents.'

'She is.' Sandra was Rachel's regular babysitter; a sixteen-year-old who lived in the village, she was always glad to earn some extra pocket money. 'As a matter of fact, my mother is coming to stay for a few days. She should be here by lunchtime. I'm sure she won't object if I pop out for a couple of hours. And I assumed you'd rather we didn't have an audience.'

Simon rubbed his jaw. 'You never told me your mother was coming.'

'Oh, for heaven's sake!' Rachel was losing all patience. 'I didn't know myself. Not until this morning. She rang me out of the blue—from the airport, would you believe? I did tell you she was visiting my brother David in New Zealand, didn't I? Well, she got back earlier than I expected, and she's decided she'd rather come and stay with us for a few days than go home. There: that's the whole story.'

Simon sniffed. 'Are you sure you didn't invite her here because you're finding Leeming too hard to handle on your own?' he muttered in an undertone, but Rachel's furious expression had him raising a placating hand. 'I didn't mean that,' he apologised hurriedly. 'Of course I believe you. You've never lied to me yet. But when I found out he was here, in the village—well, can you blame me if I jumped to the obvious conclusion?'

Rachel sighed. He had a point, and were it not for her awareness of her surroundings she'd probably have responded to his accusations with less heat.

'Tonight, hmm?' was all she said in answer, and his bluff face creased into a rueful smile.

'So long as your mother doesn't mind you leaving her on her first evening back in England,' he agreed, touching her cheek with a possessive finger. 'If she does, I suppose we'll have to humour her. I wouldn't want to fall out with my future in-laws before I've even got you living under my roof.'

Rachel managed a smile, but as Simon went jauntily out of the door she couldn't help thinking how naïve he was in some ways, if not in others. Mrs Collins had made no secret of the fact that Simon was not her ideal prospective husband for her daughter. She considered him both pompous and overbearing, and she lost no opportunity to belittle him in Rachel's eyes.

Rachel had no doubt that her mother would have plenty to say on the subject of her engagement, none of it constructive, she was sure. If only she could have had a little more time to get used to the idea herself, she thought. She was not looking forward to having to defend her decision to anyone.

And, with Ben on hand, it was going to be doubly awkward. Natural allies, he and her mother were bound to share a similar point of view. It was amazing how selective her mother's memory could be when it suited her. She'd apparently forgotten what Ben had done.

She went home at lunchtime, and to her intense annoyance Ben's Mercedes was once again parked in the drive. She was tempted to ram the back of it with her small Volkswagen, but, looking at the other car's heavy fender, she had little doubt she would come off worst.

Besides, it was no good letting Ben see he could rile her so easily. If she constantly behaved as if his being here upset her, he was bound to get the wrong impression. But remembering what had happened that morning made it difficult to behave in any normal way. No matter what she told herself, she was vulnerable.

Which was one reason why she was glad she was going out that evening. The sooner Ben—and her mother—realised she was serious about her relationship with Simon, the quicker they would come to terms with it. She refused to take his threats about Daisy seriously.

Children—especially little girls—always lived with their mother. He couldn't take her away; he wouldn't. It was just a cruel attempt to make her come to heel.

All the same, she couldn't deny the sense of apprehension she felt, when she entered the house and heard Ben and Daisy laughing together in the kitchen. She had the weirdest sense of *déjà vu*, and she wondered how many times she had come home and heard that so-familiar sound. Once, she would have shed her coat and joined them happily, eager to know what it was they were laughing about. But now, although she removed her jacket and hung it on the newel post, she hung back from entering the kitchen. She didn't want to see Daisy and her father together. She didn't want to feel any sense of guilt because she was making the final break.

In the event, she didn't have to make a formal entrance. Ben must have heard her come in, because he appeared in the kitchen doorway, a tea-towel tucked about his waist, a wooden spatula in his hand.

'Oh, hi,' he said, almost as if it was he who lived here and she was the visitor. 'I thought I heard someone in the hall.'

Rachel's lips tightened. 'Who did you expect? My mother?'

The implications of that association were so obvious, to her at least, that for a moment she was appalled at her own paranoia. What price Simon's neurotic accusations now? she thought wryly. If she wasn't careful, she'd be as suspicious as he was.

'Your mother?' echoed Ben blankly, as Daisy appeared behind him, a pinafore covering her track suit.

'D'you want some lunch, Mum?' she asked. 'Daddy's making pancakes. They didn't serve them at the hotel, and you know how much I love them.'

'How nice.' Rachel's response was sarcastic, but she couldn't help it. It was difficult not to feel resentful in the circumstances, and Ben's assumption that he could come and go as he pleased filled her with a growing sense of desperation.

'What's this about your mother?'

Clearly, Ben had not been diverted by Daisy's innocent intervention, and the little girl's eyes widened as she took in what had been said. 'Nana?' she exclaimed. 'Is Nana back from New Zealand?' She looked up at her father. 'Nana's been spending a holiday with Uncle David and Auntie Ruth. Did Mummy tell you?'

'Your mother tells me nothing,' replied Ben flatly, and then, with his eyes still on Rachel's face, 'Is your mother here?'

Rachel felt suddenly weary. 'Yes. Well—no, not yet,' she muttered distractedly, too exhausted to tell him anything but the truth. 'She phoned me from the airport this morning. She was planning on getting the morning train from Paddington. She apparently wants to prolong her holiday by staying with us.'

'Oh, whoopee!' Daisy's shriek of delight filled the empty silence. 'I wonder what she's brought me,' she added, with typical single-mindedness. 'I hope it's a koala bear. They're ever so soft and fluffy. Melanie Carpenter had one at school——'

'Koalas are from Australia,' said Rachel automatically, but Ben was still determined to have an answer.

'Why should you think I would know your mother was coming down here today?' he demanded, as Rachel endeavoured to look beyond him, into the kitchen. 'I haven't seen your mother in God knows how long. Or am I supposed to be a mind-reader? Forgive me, but didn't you just say you didn't know she was coming until this morning?'

'I don't want to talk about it.' Rachel had quickly realised her mistake, and was eager to distract his attention from it. 'I think your pancakes are burning,' she added, pointing at the cooker, but Ben barely glanced at the smoking pan.

'I get it,' he said abruptly. 'You think I've recruited your mother as an ally. You think it was my idea that she's coming to stay.' He shook his head. 'Give me a break!' He gave a short laugh. 'Your mother's too fly an old bird for that.'

Rachel's lips tightened. 'My mother is not an old bird,' she retorted coldly and, making a decision, she pushed past him into the kitchen. Removing the pan to a safe place, she opened a window to let out the smoke. Then, with the support of the sink behind her, she gestured at the messy trail of flour and milk and egg-white that decorated the table. 'I trust you intend to clean this place up. I can't afford a housekeeper.'

'Oh, Mum!'

Unfortunately, it was Daisy who felt the sharp edge of her mother's tongue, and Rachel was sorry about that. Ben, of course merely arched one dark brow in cool awareness, and she was humiliatingly conscious of his undisguised contempt.

'Don't I pay you enough?' he enquired, immediately consigning a mercenary tag to her complaint, and Rachel's nails dug into her palms. It was so easy for him; so easy to ridicule her grievances and set her down. He did it without any effort, knowing that with Daisy there she was unlikely to make a fuss.

'I'm not blaming you, sweetheart,' she said, putting an arm around the little girl's shoulders. Daisy was endeavouring to blot up the spillage with kitchen towels, and she looked at her mother with some relief.

'It's me she's getting at,' put in Ben drily, injecting a note of humour into his voice for the child's benefit. He leant past Rachel to pick up the bowl of batter, and gave it a rueful look. 'I guess we'll have to abandon these for today, small fry. I'll get Mrs Cornwell to make some, next time you come to stay.'

'Oh—must we?'

Daisy sounded plaintive, and Rachel, who was struggling to ignore the fact that she was not indifferent to Ben's nearness, snatched the bowl out of his grasp.

'I can make pancakes,' she said, even though the very idea of doing anything under her husband's eyes, when her hands were shaking, and she was in danger of spilling hot oil all over the floor, should have filled her with dismay. But anything was better than continuing this stand-off, when looking at him plumbed the dark depths of her soul.

'Did I say you couldn't?'

Ben was looking at her again, and she had the uneasy feeling that nothing he said could be taken at face value. His expression was enigmatic now, his dark eyes veiled and guarded. They made her shiver, in spite of the heat in the kitchen, and it was with real relief that she turned to the cooker.

So much for her intention of running a Hoover over the living-room carpet, and making up the spare bed for her mother, she thought, ladling a spoonful of batter into the hot pan. She didn't really have time for this. Her lunchtimes were always short and fairly frantic. It wasn't as if she cared if Mrs Cornwell was a cordon bleu chef. Once again, she had let her feelings get the better of her, and Ben probably knew that and was enjoying her frustration.

With Daisy occupied in setting the end of the kitchen table for herself and her father, Ben came to stand beside her, looking down into the bubbling pan. 'I gather you don't approve of us using your kitchen,' he said softly, breaking a corner off one of the pancakes already made and keeping warm under the hob, and popping it into his mouth. 'Hmm, these are good. Much better than I could make.'

'It's your mixture,' retorted Rachel ungraciously, as she deposited another *crepe* on the plate. 'And I don't object to anything Daisy does in this house. She has as much right to it as me. It's her home.'

'But not mine,' Ben observed quietly, helping himself to another piece of crisp pancake. 'Tell me, exactly when are you planning to move in with Mr Barrass?'

Rachel's head jerked in his direction. 'Don't you know?' she demanded coldly, realising Daisy must have supplied Simon's name.

'If I did, I wouldn't be asking,' retorted Ben smoothly. 'How many of these are you making? I don't suppose any of us will eat more than a couple.'

'Are you expecting me to believe you haven't been pumping Daisy for information?' Rachel countered, ladling another measure of batter into the pan.

'No, I'm telling you you're making too many pancakes,' replied Ben, with annoying deviation. 'I made too much batter. Shall I pour the rest away?'

'Then how do you know Simon's surname? I didn't tell you. Or have you been gossiping about me to Charlie Braddock at the Swan?'

Ben sighed. 'As a matter of fact Daisy did tell me——'

'I knew it!'

'—but not because I asked her,' finished Ben evenly. 'Apparently, that's what she calls him.' His thin lips twisted. 'I'd have expected *Uncle* Simon, at least.'

Rachel's face was red, and it wasn't just the heat from the stove. 'Unlike you, I wanted to be certain before I introduced Simon as her new *stepfather*,' she retorted scathingly. 'I can't imagine how many *aunties* she's met at Elton Square!'

Ben wasn't perturbed. 'Hasn't she told you?'

Rachel shook her head. 'No.'

'Why not?'

'I haven't asked her,' she exclaimed, although that wasn't precisely true. She had asked Daisy about who she met when she visited her father in London. The fact that no female—other than Mrs Cornwell—had figured in her narrative didn't mean there hadn't been any. Daisy could be economical with the truth too when it suited her.

Ben's expression was carefully blank now, but she doubted he believed her excuses any more than she believed his. He was still waiting for her to answer his question, and pretending she had forgotten was just playing into his hands.

And with her mother due to arrive at any time...

'Shall I set a place for Nana?' As if reading her mother's thoughts, Daisy chose that moment to look up from her attempts to fold one of the table napkins into a water lily. 'Do you think she'll like pancakes? Will there be enough?'

'Oh, yes, there'll be enough,' said Rachel quickly, glad of the breathing space. She gave her daughter a rueful grimace. 'But I don't know if she'll want any. You know how Nana worries about her figure.'

'Oh, yes.'

Daisy smiled, and resumed her efforts at origami just as Rachel realised that in her haste to speak to her daughter she had inadvertently splashed batter on to Ben's shirt. There was a wet smear of the milky liquid decorating the front of the navy blue silk shirt, and she caught her breath automatically as her anxious eyes sought his.

'Oh, God, I'm sorry,' she muttered, snatching up a tea-towel, and then hesitating over what she ought to do with it. Dabbing it dry wasn't going to be very effective, and asking him to take the shirt off so that she could wash it was simply beyond her.

'It doesn't matter,' he assured her patiently, and then, grasping her wrist, he drew the hand holding the tea-towel to his chest. With what she felt was deliberate sexuality, he made her rub the surface damage away, retaining his hold on her wrist as she did so, holding her gaze, too, until she dragged her eyes away.

'There—that's much better, don't you think?' he remarked when she'd finished, and, aware that any violent struggle to free herself might frighten Daisy, Rachel didn't argue. She simply stared in stony silence at the darker stain, still visible in spite of her efforts, wishing she'd had her lunch at work, wishing her mother would appear and save her.

'Don't you agree?' he persisted, his breath fanning the damp curls of hair that had escaped on to her forehead. The scent of his body—warm and clean and essentially male—drifted to her nostrils. 'You can wash it for me later,' he added, his thumb moving sensuously against her skin. 'I'd take it off now, but we wouldn't want your mother to come and find me half-naked. She might get the wrong impression.'

'I doubt it,' said Rachel, stung into a retort. She knew he was just tormenting her, but that didn't prevent the gibe from finding its mark. 'Will you let me go now— please? I'd like to get on with what I'm doing.'

'In a minute.' Ben directed a swift sideways glance at his daughter and then continued softly, but with definite menace, 'If you think that because I object to your ideas of moving in with Barrass he can move in here instead, think again.'

Rachel caught her breath. 'Simon wouldn't move in here,' she hissed coldly, and then, because Daisy had looked up again, she pasted an artificial smile on her face. 'He wouldn't even *sleep* in your house,' she added triumphantly. 'And don't think I haven't asked him, be- cause I have!'

But it wasn't true. For all her fierce bravado, Rachel still hadn't got over the abhorrence she felt towards sleeping with another man.

Initially, she had told herself it was because she was afraid of getting pregnant again, but that wasn't true either. A talk with a doctor soon after the separation— and some careful counselling—had convinced her that part of the problem she had had when she was living with Ben had been due to her own desperate longing to have another baby. The miscarriages—and her subsequent fear of conception—had all been explained to her, and she knew there was no reason now why she shouldn't have another child.

Another excuse she had given herself for not going to bed with Simon was that finding Ben and the au pair together had temporarily destroyed her own sexuality. But, once again, she was afraid that was very far from the truth. When Ben touched her—as he had touched her that morning—she had trouble controlling the very emotions she had previously believed were dead. Or if not dead, then frozen, she conceded ruefully. Yet Ben had awakened them, and left her more confused than ever.

The trouble was, he knew her too well, she decided irritably. They had lived together for more than eight years, after all, and that was bound to give him an advantage. That, and the fact that he enjoyed tormenting her, she thought, wondering what he was thinking at this moment. Had she really convinced him that she and Simon were lovers? Or was he simply thinking of some other way he could turn her words against her?

'Why don't you sit down?' she exclaimed now, loud enough for Daisy to hear. 'We don't want the food to get cold.'

'There's not much chance of that,' replied Ben pleasantly, leaning past her to take the dish of pancakes from the hob. His arm brushed the side of her breast as he did so, and she flinched as if he'd struck her. 'So when do I get to meet this paragon of all the virtues?' he murmured, as she turned her scarlet face towards him. 'If he's succeeded in getting into your bed, then he's obviously smarter than I thought.'

'Get stuffed!' choked Rachel rudely, and, pressing a trembling hand to her mouth, she stalked painfully out of the room.

CHAPTER SEVEN

IT WAS the rattle of teacups that awakened her.

For a moment, Rachel lay there, feeling totally disorientated. No one brought her tea to bed these days. Daisy was too young, and in any case she'd been warned not to handle boiling water.

There was a fleeting second when she wondered if everything that had happened had all been just a dream, and that what she could hear was Ben, bringing the morning tea, as he'd often done in the old days. A pot of Earl Grey, some hot buttered toast, and the morning papers—bliss! But her mother's voice dispelled that notion as quickly as it had been born.

'Really, you should be bringing my tea,' Mrs Collins remarked, coming into the bedroom in her dressing-gown, carrying the tray of teapot and cups that had woken her daughter. 'Do you realise it's after eight? Or isn't that child going to school again this morning?'

Rachel groaned, and hauled herself up on the pillows. 'Oh, God!' she said, staring at the bedside clock with some disbelief. 'Is that the time? Daisy's bus will be along in twenty minutes. And she takes an age in the bathroom, not to mention getting her breakfast——'

'Relax.' Her mother settled herself comfortably on the end of the bed and deposited the tray beside her. 'Daisy's up and dressed, and having her breakfast right at this minute.' She grimaced wryly. 'The advantages of jet-lag. I've been awake since five o'clock.'

Lucky you! thought Rachel ruefully, but she didn't say it. She guessed it had been around that time that she'd fallen asleep. 'Thanks, Mum,' she offered, accepting the cup of tea Mrs Collins had poured her with gratitude. The knowledge that she didn't have to go tearing out of bed was a positive blessing. The way she felt this morning, she could have happily pulled the covers over her head and stayed where she was.

'So,' said her mother, after they had sipped their tea in silence for a few minutes, 'what are you going to do?'

Rachel shrugged. 'Drink this, get up, and go to work, I suppose,' she replied, deliberately misunderstanding her. 'What are you going to do? I don't want you to spend your time as an unpaid housekeeper. This place may not be the showplace you'd like to see it, but it is clean, and I do everything that's necessary in the evening and at weekends.'

Mrs Collins let her finish, and then she repeated her question. 'I meant, what are you going to do about Ben,' she essayed, lifting her eyes from the teacup. 'As far as I can see, you've got quite a problem on your hands, and you're not going to resolve it by burying your head in the sand.'

Rachel was indignant. 'I'm not burying my head in the sand?'

'Well, I think you are. If you'd really wanted to get the situation settled, you'd have invited your pig-farmer in last night, instead of scuttling off to meet him at the gate.'

Rachel took a deep breath. 'How many more times——?'

'I know, I know.' But her mother didn't sound repentant. 'He's not a pig-farmer. But he is a farmer, isn't he? And if you want everybody to take you seriously, then you should put your cards on the table.'

'I wish you'd stop talking in clichés, Mother. And why should you think I don't want to be taken seriously, just because I choose to avoid unnecessary rows? I have Daisy to consider. I can't invite Simon in here while Ben's at home. You know what would happen, and I won't take the risk.'

'At home,' echoed her mother drily. 'You said—while Ben's at home. Does that mean you still regard this as Ben's home?'

'Of course not.' Rachel was angry that she had made such an obvious *faux pas*. 'But it's still his house, isn't it?' She gathered a little confidence from her mother's doubtful expression, and hurried on, 'He's made no secret of the fact that he doesn't want Simon here.' That, at least, was true. 'And I don't see why I should subject Simon to his particular kind of baiting. Not when there's no need for it. Not when I intend to deal with Ben through our respective solicitors from now on.'

Mrs Collins frowned. 'Is that wise?'

'Is what wise?' Rachel was getting more disgruntled by the minute. The welcome cup of tea was having its price, after all, and she was beginning to wish she had set the alarm as she usually did. But last night she had been too tense, too fraught, to think coherently. She'd been sure she wouldn't sleep in any case, and she hadn't been far wrong.

'Dealing with Ben through a solicitor,' replied her mother now, evidently determined to have her say. 'I don't want to interfere——'

'Then don't!'

'—but I have to say, I don't think Ben will like it. And as there's Daisy to consider, it might pay to keep him sweet.'

'To keep him sweet!' Rachel stared at her mother as if she'd taken leave of her senses. 'Mum, I don't have to "keep him sweet". As a matter of fact, I don't care how he feels. And if he's been regaling you with his idea of taking me to court then I'm sorry, but I won't be threatened.'

'Taking you to court?' Her mother's frown deepened. 'Well, of course you'll have to go to court, if you want the divorce to be legal.'

'I know that.' Rachel felt as if she was wading through deeper and deeper water, when all she really wanted to

do was get into the shallows. 'I meant take me to court
about Daisy. Ben's threatened to sue for custody, if I go
to live with Simon.'

'Go to live with Simon?' Mrs Collins looked even more
confused, and Rachel wished she'd never started this.
'You mean—after you and this man are married? Why
should he do that? Unless he thinks there's some reason
why she shouldn't live in the same house as——'

'It's not that!' Rachel heaved a sigh. 'Oh, you might
as well know; Simon has suggested we go to live at
Kingsmead while we're waiting for the divorce to be made
final.'

Her mother's lips parted. 'And you're prepared to do
this?'

'Why not?'

'Why not?' Mrs Collins gasped. 'Oh, Rachel, you can't
expect me to believe you don't know how unsuitable that
would be for Daisy! The child needs security. She needs
a stable home. And I don't mean one in a farmyard,
before you try to make a joke of it.'

'I wouldn't do that.'

'But you are prepared to jeopardise your daughter's
future, aren't you?' exclaimed her mother impatiently.
'How can you expect her to know right from wrong when
her own mother is so desperate for a man that she's
willing to take him on any terms, with or without the
sanctity of marriage.'

Rachel groaned. 'It's not like that.'

'Then what is it like?'

Rachel shook her head. 'You know, heaps of people
do it. Live together before they're married, I mean.'

'Well, I don't approve; not when there are children
involved,' declared Mrs Collins firmly. 'And nor did you,
before this—this—farmer came along.'

Rachel's lips twitched at her mother's obvious difficulty in removing the word 'pig' from Simon's
description, but it was important that she understand
exactly what was involved. Perhaps her mother could

persuade Ben that Daisy's morals were not in danger. 'There are cottages on the farm,' she explained. 'Simon wants us to go and live in one of them—only until we're married, of course. It's a few miles from Kingsmead to Upper Morton. It would be so much easier when he visited us if he didn't have a long drive home.'

'Hmm.' Mrs Collins didn't sound impressed. 'And what about you? What about the fact that you'll be that much further from the shop? And Daisy? What about Daisy? You're going to have to get up early, to get her here in time for the bus.'

Rachel lifted one hand and pushed her fingers through the tumbled mass of her hair. Now for the crunch, she thought wearily. 'Simon thinks Daisy should go to the local school, now that she's older. There's no real reason why she should travel into Cheltenham every day. She hardly knows any of the children in the village.'

Mrs Collins didn't say anything. Just when Rachel was sure she was in danger of bringing her mother's wrath down upon her head, the older woman got up from the bed, and lifting the tray, walked briskly towards the door.

'I'm sure Daisy must have finished her breakfast by now,' she said pleasantly, confounding Rachel's notions of how she'd react. 'You take your time. I can see her off. I'll send her up to say goodbye in a few minutes.'

Rachel plunked her cup down on the bedside table, and stared at her mother frustratedly. 'Is that it?' she exclaimed, unable to prevent the thwarted question, and Mrs Collins raised her brows.

'Is that what, dear? The bus? Oh, no, I don't think so. Not yet——'

'No.' Rachel knew her mother knew exactly what she was talking about, and her bland obtuseness made her want to scream. 'Don't you have anything to say about what I've just told you? Can't you see the advantages for all of us?'

'All I can see is a very selfish woman, and a man who obviously considers his own comforts before those of

anyone else,' retorted Mrs Collins, calmly shifting the
tray to one hand to enable her to close the door. 'Oh—
and Daisy asked me to remind you that you have to write
her a note. Not only about her being absent yesterday,
but whether you're going to help—Miss Gregory, is it?—
with the jumble sale next week.'

By the time Rachel came downstairs, Daisy had left for
school, and the kitchen was spotless. A bowl had been
left for her own cereal, courtesy of her daughter's instructions, she was sure. But evidently Mrs Collins had
gone to take her shower, and the only sound was that
of running water.

Rachel ground some beans and brewed a pot of coffee
while she waited, deciding that if she was late this
morning then Cyril would have to dock her pay. She
refused to leave for work without speaking to her mother
again. And with Daisy around most of the time it wasn't
always easy to have a private conversation.

She put the dish that had been left for her away, and
poured herself a mug of coffee when it was ready. She
had no appetite again, but that was hardly surprising in
the circumstances. With her whole family ganging up on
her, how was she supposed to live a normal life?

Mrs Collins appeared as she was draining her second
cup, and in spite of her misgivings about the older
woman's interpretation of current events she couldn't
help the rueful thought that this morning her mother
looked—and probably felt—younger than she did.

Like her daughter, Mrs Collins' hair was the deep lus-
trous shade of a chestnut, and the liberal streaks of grey
that had appeared had only added to its appeal. Unlike
her daughter, she wore her hair short and had it permed
occasionally. In consequence, it was soft and wavy, and
framed her fine-boned features.

Rachel had sometimes wondered if her mother had
ever thought of getting married again herself. Rachel's
father had died in a car crash when she and her brother

were very young, and it hadn't always been easy for her mother, supporting herself and her children. A windfall legacy from an elderly aunt when Rachel and David were teenagers had changed all that, however. The capital, carefully invested, had provided a generous income, and both children had gone on to university, without any of the financial restrictions that living only on a grant would have entailed. It had made her mother's need to work superfluous, too. Mrs Collins had taken a part-time job subsequently, but that had been for personal reasons, because she enjoyed the company.

'I thought you'd have gone by now,' Mrs Collins remarked, as she came into the kitchen, and Rachel wondered if she really meant that, or if it was simply a means of covering her own embarrassment. Her parting statement, after delivering the tea, had been more than a little biased, and Rachel wanted to know what grounds she had for disparaging a man she hardly knew.

'Well, as you can see...' Rachel let the words speak for themselves. 'Do you want some coffee?'

'That would be nice.'

The studied politeness was so unlike her mother's usual conviviality that Rachel half wished she had left this until later after all. She didn't want to row with her mother, and the suspicion that Ben had had at least some part in Mrs Collins' present attitude was worrying. He had been here when she'd scurried out to meet Simon the night before, and she had no way of knowing how long he'd stayed. Or what had been said, she admitted tensely. But surely her mother would take her word before that of a man who had done nothing to gain her confidence.

'What time did Ben leave last night?' she asked now, deciding she might as well know her enemy before she started. She set a second mug of coffee on the table. 'Oh—have you eaten? I never thought.'

Mrs Collins' expression implied there was a wealth of meaning behind those few words, but Rachel refused to be daunted. So far as she was concerned she'd done nothing wrong, and the sooner her mother realised that, the better.

'I had some cereal with Daisy,' the older woman replied, picking up her cup without taking the chair her daughter had pulled out for her. She essayed surprise when Rachel followed her into the living-room however. 'Oh—aren't you leaving? I thought you started at nine o'clock.'

'I do—usually,' appended Rachel drily. 'I just think we have some things to say to one another, and I thought it might be easier on both of us if Daisy wasn't listening in.'

Mrs Collins sniffed. 'Well—I did have something to tell you last evening, but what with your attitude towards Ben...' She paused. 'And then you went running off to see your farmer friend. It just didn't seem the right time.'

'I assume Ben's been enlisting your sympathies in my absence,' Rachel remarked caustically. 'Well, I shouldn't believe everything he says, if I were——'

'Did I say it was about Ben?' her mother interrupted her coolly. 'Did I give any intimation that anything your husband said had influenced me, one way or the other?'

'Well—no——'

'Then kindly stop jumping to conclusions. My interpretation of your affair with Mr Barrass owes nothing to anything Ben might have told me. The situation alone is explanation enough. Has it occurred to you, Rachel, that he may have no intention of marrying you?'

'Simon?'

'Who else?'

Rachel caught her breath. 'Mother, it was Simon who suggested I get a divorce from Ben!'

'So?'

'So he would hardly do that, if he didn't expect us to get married.'

'Are you engaged?'

'As good as.'

'Has he bought you a ring?'

'Not yet.' Rachel felt resentful. 'Mother, what is all this about? Heavens, you've only met Simon a couple of times. Why should you even think he might have some ulterior motive? I've told you it's not as if we're going to live in the main house. Daisy and I are going to occupy one of the tied cottages on the estate.'

'Huh.' Her mother snorted. 'And you don't think there's anything out of the ordinary about that? You don't think that it would have been more in keeping with his claim that he wants to marry you to allow you to remain here until your marriage? Upper Morton is a small place, Rachel, as you're so fond of telling me. What do you think people will think if you go and live at Kingsmead while you're still married to Ben?'

Rachel sighed. 'Does it matter what people think?'

'It will if you don't get married.' Her mother paused. 'Didn't you tell me he's been a bachelor all these years, and that he still lives with his mother?'

'So?'

'So, I can't imagine the old lady will take kindly to having her position usurped, can you? And once he's got you where he wants you, why should he be in any hurry to make it all legal?'

Rachel swallowed to lubricate her dry throat. 'You don't have much of an opinion of me, do you?'

'On the contrary. It's because I do care about you, whatever your faults, that I'm telling you what I think now. It's no use my waiting until you and Daisy have taken up residence at Kingsmead, is it? Once this house is sold, you won't be able to come back here. And I— well, I won't be here either.'

Rachel gulped. 'You—you're not—I mean——'

'I'm not desperately ill, if that's what you think I'm trying to say,' replied Mrs Collins drily. 'No. I've never felt better, as a matter of fact. But you must have wondered why I came home early, and why I wanted to see you before I went back to the flat.' She bit her lip, and if Rachel hadn't known better she'd have said her mother was looking rather coy now. 'As a matter of fact, I'm going to get married. I've met a man in New Zealand—David's boss, as a matter of fact. He's a widower. He has been for a number of years, just like me. I know you'll think it's sudden, but I did meet him briefly two years ago, when I visited David and Ruth.' She gazed at her daughter anxiously now. 'Don't look so staggered. I'm only fifty-three, you know.'

Rachel licked her lips. 'I'm not—staggered,' she protested.

But she was. More on account of the fact that her mother would be moving out of England. It wasn't that they had ever lived in one another's pockets; they hadn't. But Mrs Collins had always been there if she needed her. As when she'd found Ben and Elena together. Oh, God, she was going to miss her.

'You looked stunned,' remarked her mother now, seating herself on the sofa, and cradling her coffee cup between her palms. 'And—and although you may not believe this, I have consoled myself with the thought that at least you and Daisy were going to be cared for. I can't pretend to like Simon—but, as you've pointed out, I scarcely know him. Nevertheless, I am concerned at the idea of your burning your boats, so to speak, and moving to Kingsmead.' She lifted her shoulders. 'Don't do it, Rachel. Even if you won't listen to Ben, listen to me——'

'Wait a minute.' Rachel determinedly put her doubts aside and pounced on the one inconsistency in her mother's story. 'I thought you said Ben hadn't influenced you.'

'He hasn't.'

'But you did discuss this last night, didn't you? You already knew Simon had asked me to move to Kingsmead, didn't you? Oh, yes, no wonder you were so reticent on the subject of how long Ben had stayed. I bet you had a real heart-to-heart. Did he happen to tell you who he was sleeping with at the moment? Or is he allowed to do what he likes?'

'It's beautiful, isn't it?'

Cyril handed the icon to Rachel with reverential hands. The picture of St Nicholas, flanked by the twin figures of the Saviour and the Mother of God, was painted on a gold ground, and was probably worth several thousand pounds. But Rachel was in no mood to appreciate it.

'It's very nice,' she offered, half-heartedly, smoothing the raised plaque with her thumb, and Cyril gave her a glowering look.

'It's very nice,' he mimicked irritably. 'Is that all you can find to say? It's exquisite; magnificent; worth at least seven thousand pounds, at my reckoning.'

'Really?' Rachel endeavoured to inject a note of admiration into her voice. 'Where did you find it? Romanby Court?'

'Romanby Court!' Cyril scoffed at the idea. 'I didn't find any Russian items at Romanby court. No, an American brought it in earlier this morning. He originally just wanted it valued, but when I told him how valuable it was, he asked if I'd be prepared to sell it for him.'

'An American?' Rachel made an effort to put her own problems aside. 'What American? I didn't know there were any Americans living in the village.'

'There aren't.' Cyril looked a little discomforted now. 'He's staying at the Old Swan. He said he's over here, visiting some relatives in the district. One of them had asked him if there was any likelihood of them realising some cash on the icon. He offered to try a couple of dealers, and because he's staying in the village I just happened to be the first.'

In spite of her dejection, Rachel was amazed. 'You're not serious.'

'Why not?'

'You should know why not.' Rachel stared at him impatiently. 'Didn't you see that programme on television, just last week?'

'I don't watch television,' said Cyril huffily, but Rachel wasn't deterred by his aggrieved expression.

'Then you should,' she declared. 'Ever since perestroika, dozens of valuable religious relics have been smuggled into the West. Particularly icons. I hope you have some proof of where this came from. You didn't give him a cash payment, I assume.'

Cyril sniffed. 'Of course not. I'm not stupid. And as far as its provenance is concerned, he's coming back tomorrow with all the necessary papers. As I said, he's handling the matter for a member of his family. He couldn't make any promises without speaking to them first.'

Rachel frowned. 'But he left the icon with you? He left a valuable Russian icon in your hands, without any money changing hands?'

'I didn't say that.'

'As good as.'

Cyril tossed his head. 'Look here, I didn't ask for your opinion, Rachel. I thought you'd be interested, that's all.'

'But you did give him some money, didn't you?'

'A—token of my interest in the icon, yes. If I hadn't, he might have taken it to some other dealer. It's not on any list of stolen items, or—*hot*, as they say in the business. I had to give him something, as he was willing to leave the icon with me. It was only five hundred pounds. That was all the cash I had.'

'Five hundred pounds!' Rachel shook her head. 'What was wrong with a cheque?'

'He was short of cash——'

'I bet he was.'

'There's no need to be so sarcastic, Rachel. This is my shop, you know. If I choose to do business with a client of my choosing, I don't think you have anything to do with it.'

'All right.'

Her initial surge of concern on Cyril's behalf subdued, Rachel felt a returning sense of gloom as her own worries reasserted themselves. For a few moments, she had allowed herself to be diverted by Cyril's greed. But now, she was forced to concede that it wasn't really her problem. 'No one—and I mean no one—would accept five hundred pounds for a valuable item like this,' Cyril added, proving he was not as sanguine about the situation as he had stated.

'How do you know?' Rachel shrugged. 'How do you know it's as valuable as you say? How often have you handled Russian icons?'

'Not very often, as you know,' said Cyril, who had never handled one in Rachel's recollection. 'Anyway, what does it matter? If he doesn't come back, I shall sell it. Even you must admit it's worth more than the money I gave him.'

'Oh, yes. It's worth more. Probably much more,' agreed Rachel, nodding. 'But whatever you say, you've no proof it wasn't smuggled into this country. And if it was, or if you even suspect that it was, you have to inform the police. Unless you want to run the risk of being accused of handling stolen goods.'

Cyril sniffed. 'Well, I'm prepared to give the chap the benefit of the doubt. As I say, he's staying at the Swan at the moment. I saw him in the bar there last night. Your husband's a guest at the hotel, too. Perhaps you could ask him if he's spoken to him. I'd be interested to hear Ben's opinion.'

'Oh, no!' Rachel held up her hand, palm outwards. 'Don't ask me to get involved in this.' She paused. 'Besides, I—believe Ben is going back to London this morning.'

'I don't think so.' Cyril looked smug now. 'I had a few words with him myself last night, and from what he said I think he's planning on staying a couple of weeks.'

CHAPTER EIGHT

'DID you know Ben was planning on staying in the village?' Rachel asked her mother that evening, after Daisy had gone upstairs to watch a cartoon programme on the television. They had all had an early meal, to enable Daisy to eat with them, and now Mrs Collins was helping her daughter load their dirty plates into the dishwasher. The machine hadn't been used for ages. Rachel generally just rinsed hers and Daisy's dishes at the sink. But her mother had prepared the meal for them, and consequently there were many more items than usual.

'No.'

Mrs Collins was offhand, as she'd been ever since Rachel came home. The fact that her daughter hadn't come home at lunchtime might be the cause, but Rachel suspected otherwise. The altercation they had had before she left for work that morning was more likely the culprit, but she doubted her mother would believe her if she told her that she hadn't stayed away deliberately.

'Anyway, thanks for being here when Daisy came home,' she said now, reaching for the washing fluid. 'What did you do all day?'

'This and that.' Mrs Collins wouldn't be drawn. 'Aren't you putting too much of that powder in the reservoir?' she remarked obliquely. 'This water is very soft. You don't want to waste the stuff, the price it is nowadays.'

Rachel immediately stopped filling the container, and set the plastic bottle aside. It wasn't that long since she'd used the dishwasher that she didn't remember how much cleanser to use. But she had no wish to start an argument with her mother based on nothing more than a household matter. They had plenty of other problems. Not least, their disagreement over Simon.

If Simon himself was offended by her mother's attitude, he had chosen to ignore it. Last night, he had been more concerned with the reasons why Ben was still in the village. And it hadn't been easy, explaining why her husband had chosen to come to Upper Morton, rather than dealing with the matter through his solicitors. But, much to her surprise, Simon hadn't questioned her reasons for rushing out to meet him, instead of inviting him in to discuss the problem, man-to-man. In his opinion, he and Ben had nothing to say to one another.

'Anyway, he's mainly come to see Daisy,' Rachel had volunteered quickly, telling herself she was glad Simon was taking it this way. The last thing she'd wanted was for Ben and Simon to come to blows over her. Well—over Daisy, she'd amended ruefully. Ben was unlikely to fight for something he hadn't cared about in the first place.

'He's not going to make it easy though, is he?' Simon exclaimed, as they sat in his Range Rover, overlooking the darkening valley below Crag's Leap. At any time of the day or night the rocky promontory was a popular beauty spot, but even the winking lights below them couldn't rally Rachel's spirits tonight.

'He's not made any comment, one way or the other,' she replied, consoling her conscience with the thought that so far as the divorce was concerned, she wasn't lying. 'It was just—a shock for him, I expect. We have been living apart for quite some time.'

'All the more reason why he should have anticipated this happening,' retorted Simon shortly. 'For heaven's sake, does he think he's the only one who's entitled to have an extra-marital relationship? You're not a nun, Rachel. Though——' she saw his thick lips twist slightly in the light from the dashboard '—I could be forgiven for wondering.'

Rachel had winced at his choice of words. Winced, too, at his less-than-discreet way of reminding her that she was still keeping him at arm's length. And why should Ben behave as if what she was suggesting was immoral? He had spent the last three years proving he was definitely no saint.

'It'll be different when—when we're married,' she'd said, and as if realising he had been rather tactless Simon had gathered her close in his arms.

'I hope I won't have to wait that long,' he'd said, nuzzling his lips against her neck. 'But don't worry——' this, as she'd stiffened '—no one's going to hurry you. I know how much that bastard hurt you. All I want to do is show you how much I love you. And make you forget Ben Leeming, and his dirty little affairs.'

Now, Rachel put the memory of that conversation with Simon aside. At least one person wanted her happiness above all else. She mustn't let her mother—or Ben— spoil that. Or allow them to twist his words so that she started doubting his intentions.

'Have—er—have you seen Ben today?' she asked, after the dishwasher was happily humming away, and her mother gave her a neutral look.

'Does it matter? Does whether or not I see my son-in-law have anything to do with you in the present circumstances?'

'Oh, Mum!' Rachel sighed. 'Do we have to have an argument, just because I've asked a perfectly innocent question? Naturally I'm interested. And naturally it has something to do with me. I want to know if he mentioned the divorce.'

'Mmm, well...' Her mother frowned. 'Shall we go into the other room, or are you rushing out again?'

Rachel contained the retort that sprang to her lips at the unfair question, and took a deep breath. 'By all means,' she said, 'let's make ourselves comfortable. And I won't be—rushing out again, as you put it. I want to hear about your holiday. That is, if we can stop all this sniping.'

Mrs Collins shrugged, and as she followed her into the lamplit family-room Rachel acknowledged that she'd welcome a break in hostilities. It seemed as if she had done nothing else but defend herself ever since she made that phone call to Ben.

And, as a matter of fact, she had made no plans for the evening. When Simon had called, she had explained that she wanted to spend the evening with her mother. She owed it to her, she said, to make as much of the time they had left as possible, and when Simon found out why he had been unexpectedly understanding. A less sympathetic ear might have detected a note of relief in his willingness to concede, but Rachel refused to read anything unworthy into his compliance. The thought that her mother's moving to New Zealand removed another obstacle from his path was born of Mrs Collins' accusations, not of anything he had done. And mothers-in-law always presented a problem. She knew: she'd have Simon's mother to deal with.

'So,' she said, after they were seated, 'have you seen Ben?'

Her mother hesitated. 'We had lunch together, yes.'

'Lunch?' Rachel felt an unnecessary twinge of resentment. 'How nice.'

'Yes, it was, actually.' Mrs Collins regarded her daughter with a shrewd eye. 'It was a pity that you couldn't join us. The home-made quiches at the Heronry are quite delicious.'

Rachel's brows drew together. 'You went to the Heronry?' The Heronry was a well-known eating place near Cheltenham, small, but expensive. It was usually impossible to get a table at short notice.

'Yes.' Her mother looked smug. 'One of the advantages of having a name people recognise. I remember what you told me about trying to book a table there. Well, let me tell you, its reputation is very well deserved.'

Rachel moistened her lower lip. 'I'm glad you enjoyed yourself.' She paused, and then, realising she had sounded rather peevish, she added hastily, 'I assumed you'd eaten here or at the Swan.'

'Hmm.' Mrs Collins nodded. 'A natural mistake. But Ben was never stingy with his money, was he? You've never gone short of anything, even though you threw him out.'

Rachel gasped. 'I didn't throw him out. Mother, you may have forgotten——'

'I haven't forgotten anything. And nor has Ben. I really think you should talk to him, Rachel. Before you do anything irrevocable.'

Rachel could hardly speak. 'He's really got you fooled, hasn't he?' she exclaimed at last. 'And don't think I didn't notice the dig about Simon. And, for your information, I'm not as well off as you think. Sometimes I find it very hard to pay all the bills, and just because Ben supports Daisy, you shouldn't think he's generous with me.'

Mrs Collins looked disturbed. 'Why haven't you told me this before?'

'Because I didn't want to worry you.'

'Does Ben know?'

'It's nothing to do with Ben.'

'I disagree.' The older woman frowned. 'Why, he was only saying this lunchtime that he'd have to increase your allowance.'

'Not *my* allowance, Daisy's allowance,' said Rachel shortly, not really wanting to get into this. The fact that Ben *had* offered to pay her bills too was a constant source of annoyance. She didn't want to take anything more from him than she had to, and it irritated her to think that he was giving her mother the impression that he still controlled her finances.

'Well, why don't you explain——?'

Rachel glared at her mother. 'Mother, how many more times must I say it? I don't want Ben's help. I don't want anything from him. No, correction: I do want a divorce. Now, are you going to tell me whether he mentioned it, or shall we just talk about David and Ruth, and this new man in your life?'

Mrs Collins sniffed. 'Well, of course he mentioned it.'

'And?'

'He doesn't want a divorce.'

Rachel expelled her breath slowly. 'It doesn't really matter what he wants.'

'It does. If you hope to retain custody of Daisy.' Mrs Collins paused, and then added earnestly, 'I have to say it again, Rachel, I don't think it's very wise to try and precipitate the issue.'

'By moving to Kingsmead?'

'That—and other things.'

'What other things?'

'Well—by attempting to move Daisy to another school.'

'Did you tell him that?'

'I didn't *tell* him anything,' retorted her mother drily. 'That's my own personal opinion. I just think you should consider very carefully before making a decision. He hasn't said he'll oppose the divorce, but I wouldn't do anything rash.'

Rachel's stomach hollowed. 'Has he made any threats?'

'Oh, Rachel,' Mrs Collins looked cross now. 'Ben doesn't make threats. Not to me anyway,' she amended, observing her daughter's expression. 'I'm sure he has your best interests at heart. Just as I have.'

Rachel's lips twisted. 'How sweet!'

'Well, if you're going to take that attitude...'

Mrs Collins looked as if she was about to get up from her chair, and Rachel hastily made her peace. 'I'm not,' she said unhappily. 'I know you mean well, and I'm not getting at you, honestly. I'd just like to know why Ben's come here. I don't believe—I can't believe—it's just to protect Daisy's interests.'

* * *

Rachel was leaving the post office when the sleek lines of her husband's Mercedes cruised to a halt beside her. For a moment she thought Ben wanted something from the shop, which was a post office and general dealer's combined, but when he leant across the front seat and pushed open the nearside door she realised she had been mistaken.

Her impulse was to walk on, but Cyril was watching from the window of his shop next door. Ever since their altercation over the Russian icon at the end of last week he had been watching her like a hawk, waiting for her to make some error he could pounce on. The fact that the helpful stranger hadn't come back, and that Cyril had had to report the matter to the local constabulary, had left him in a very tetchy mood; and Rachel had no intention of feeding his delight at her discomposure by appearing flustered.

'Get in. I'll give you a lift,' Ben ordered, and although she was loath to accept his offer Rachel only hesitated a moment before doing as he suggested. She had been on her feet for the better part of nine hours, and she was ready to take a rest.

But not with him, she thought irritably, having heard enough of him from Daisy during the past couple of days. The little girl had spent most of the weekend with her father, and, while Rachel was glad she hadn't brought him to the house again, the fact that they'd been together was provocation enough at present.

Of course, she wouldn't have been put in this position if she hadn't loaned her mother her car. But it had seemed pointless leaving the Volkswagen standing outside the shop all day when Mrs Collins could use it. She'd been planning on going into Cheltenham today, and right now Rachel wished she were with her.

As soon as she was inside the car and the door closed, Ben took off at speed. Within seconds, they had reached the turn for Stoneberry Lane, but instead of slowing down he accelerated, and it didn't take any feat of intelligence to realise he had no intention of taking her home.

'Had a good day?' he enquired, when it became obvious that, in spite of her fury, she wasn't going to say anything, and Rachel turned her head.

'Where are you taking me?'

'To see a house.' Ben's answer was as startling as the feathering of moisture that enveloped her skin when he looked at her. 'You're pale,' he added, and she immediately felt as colourless as a sheet. His dark eyes alighted on her hands, clasped together tightly in her lap. 'Relax,' he advised softly. 'I told your mother I'd pick you up.'

Rachel swallowed the indignation she felt that her mother hadn't considered it important enough to advise her of his intentions. She turned her head and looked out of the window. Beyond the burgeoning hedgerows, lambs were playing in the fields, and although it was early evening the sun was still quite warm. She had been looking forward to going home. Maybe spending an undemanding hour in the garden. The greenhouse still needed cleaning, and she ought to sort some jumble out for the sale next weekend.

'Aren't you speaking?'

Ben's voice invaded her thoughts, and try as she might she couldn't ignore it. With some reluctance, she cast a brief glance in his direction. In black jeans and a black Oxford shirt, he should have looked sombre, but he didn't. It was she, in her neat white blouse and navy skirt, with her hair drawn tightly back into its usual braid, who appeared stiff and unforgiving. Relaxed behind the wheel, his arm resting casually on the window, he looked half amused, and dangerously familiar. His expression was decidedly whimsical, and she wondered what he'd really come here for.

'What am I supposed to say?' she asked now, realising as she did so that her voice sounded sharp and peevish. Not at all what he was used to, she was sure.

But telling her he was taking her to see a house was surely the poorest excuse imaginable.

He shrugged now, his shoulders moving smoothly beneath the soft cotton of his shirt. 'Tell me about your day,' he suggested evenly. 'Is Cyril still running you ragged? Is that why you look so tired sometimes?'

'No!' Rachel glared at him indignantly, wishing she wasn't so aware of his superb physical condition. 'If I look tired, it's not Cyril's fault, it's yours. I haven't done much sleeping since you barged back into my life.'

Ben's mouth twitched. 'Why do I get the feeling that that's not as complimentary as it sounds?'

'Because it's not.' Rachel was quick to disabuse him of any ambiguity in her words. 'You know perfectly well I don't want you here. And if you think enlisting my mother's help is going to change that, you'd better think again.'

Ben eased himself into a more comfortable position, adjusting the tight denim between his legs, and running an assessing hand along his thigh. Rachel could have ignored it. She would have ignored it, she told herself, but her initial reaction to his movement was one of unadulterated panic. She'd thought he was going to touch her. She'd thought his shifting in his seat had heralded another assault on her emotions. And that was something she couldn't allow. She was too afraid of the aftermath.

'Am I responsible for this?' he asked at last, when she was drawn into the corner of her seat, her arms wrapped about her middle, her knees pressed tightly together, and Rachel cast him a fulminating look.

'Why don't you just take me home?' she demanded angrily, as frustrated by her own reaction as his. 'We have nothing more to say to say to one another.'

'Where have I heard that before?' Ben braked behind a trundling tractor, and regarded her tolerantly. 'As I see it, I haven't said half enough. I thought I had more time. But——' he paused '—I find I haven't.'

'I don't know what you're talking about.' But the relief at finding he wasn't about to touch her had taken the edge from her voice. 'Why don't we let the solicitors deal with it? I'm sure they've got more time, and they've certainly got more interest.'

'I disagree.' Ben drew her unwilling gaze back to him. 'Anything you do interests me. That's why I'm here.'

'Stuff your interest,' said Rachel rudely, annoyed to find her hands were still trembling. Oh, God, why did he always have this effect on her? Why couldn't she ignore him, as he'd ignored her for the past two years?

Ben's smile was indulgent. Evidently she wasn't going to make any headway by being childish. But she'd known that already. It was just so difficult to be objective with him.

The tractor was in no hurry, and nor was Ben, apparently. The powerful Mercedes idled along behind the lumbering machine, making no attempt to overtake, even though the road ahead was perfectly clear. Rachel's nerves stretched to screaming pitch at this deliberate waste of her free time. It was all right for him; he didn't have to work five days out of seven.

Then, just as she was contemplating the wisdom of opening her door and jumping out, the reason for Ben's patience was explained. As she was calculating the time it would take for him to turn the Mercedes in the narrow road and come after her, they turned off on to an even narrower lane. She glimpsed a signpost that said Watersmeet, but she'd never heard of it. But then, there were dozens of villages in these parts that barely warranted a pinprick on the map.

'Where are we going?' she demanded, realising now exactly how helpless she was. Unless he chose to take her back, it was going to be very difficult to find her way home unaided. She could always phone her mother, of course. But Mrs Collins was hopelessly inept at reading a map.

'I've told you,' he replied, as the Mercedes glided easily over a rise in the road. 'I'm taking you to see a house. It's not far now, I promise.'

Rachel pressed her lips together. She realised it was pointless telling him she didn't want to see the house— *any* house, if it came to that. She wanted to go home. Before anything awful happened.

They rounded a bend, and then swung almost immediately between stone gateposts. If there had ever been gates, they were there no longer, but the Mercedes's tyres crunched over a cattle grid before riding up a long, curving drive.

There were trees lining the drive, tall oaks and poplars, with here and there the placid beauty of a horse-chestnut. Which was appropriate really, because there were horses in the paddocks that stretched beyond the pavement, beautiful thoroughbred animals, who regarded their passage without dissent.

Rachel opened her mouth to ask who the horses belonged to, and then shut it again. She didn't want to know, she told herself. She wasn't interested. She had no wish to start a conversation with him that might be construed as giving in.

The drive meandered over a stone bridge, with a stream gurgling merrily beneath, and it became increasingly difficult to hide her admiration when the house appeared beyond a belt of trees. Mellow-bricked, and ivy-hung, it was a pretty example of a small manor house, with many long-paned windows and a central portico.

There was smoke curling from one of the many chimneys that decorated the tiled roof, and immediately Rachel felt more at ease. Whoever owned the house was evidently at home. For all her fears of an abduction, she had obviously been mistaken.

And, after all, why should Ben wish to abduct her? she thought, giving him a surreptitious look. For heaven's sake, she was letting her imagination run away with her. He'd told her mother she was with him. If she

could believe that. It wouldn't be the first time he had
lied to her.

'Like it?' he asked now, and, determinedly putting
any negative thoughts aside, Rachel nodded.

'It's beautiful,' she said, as the drive curved into a
circle of gravel, with an island fountain in its centre.
'Who does it belong to?'

Ben hesitated. 'It's owned by some people called
Armstrong,' he replied at last, and briefly the name
touched a chord in Rachel's mind. But before she could
follow it up, he brought the car to a halt before the
shallow steps leading up to the front door. 'Come on,'
he said, thrusting open his door. 'I'll show it to you. It's
got five bedrooms and three bathrooms, and a couple
of acres of garden and an orchard at the back.'

Of course, it wasn't the sort of reply she had expected. But, with Ben out of the car and gesturing to
her to follow him, she didn't have a lot of choice. Oh,
she could have remained where she was, she thought afterwards, but at the time she didn't think of it. She supposed she was still under the illusion that the Armstrongs
would be waiting for them, and when a middle-aged
woman opened the door her supposition seemed to be
confirmed.

All the same, she wished she'd had some warning of
where she was going before she left the shop. Although
she had washed her face and renewed her make-up at
lunchtime, four more hours of cataloguing, dusting, and
unpacking had taken their toll. Her hands were clean,
but she felt grubby. Why couldn't he have shown her
the house this evening, after she'd had time to change?

The answer was obvious, of course. And he had known
it. Given a choice, she would never have agreed to this
outing. Given any option, she'd have run a mile before
she put herself so recklessly into his hands.

Ben was speaking to the woman now, and, realising
she couldn't vacillate any longer, Rachel opened the
car door and got out. The casual jacket she had been

carrying when Ben pulled up beside her, she now slipped over her shoulders. A soft cream mohair, it at least gave her a semblance of self-confidence.

'This is Mrs Morris,' Ben introduced her easily. 'My wife,' he added, and Rachel knew she didn't have the nerve to contradict him. Besides, *estranged* wife would be splitting hairs, wouldn't it? She doubted Mrs Morris was interested . . .

Mrs Morris?

She gave Ben a suspicious look as the woman invited them into the house. Where was Mrs Armstrong? she wanted to ask irritably. And then it occurred to her that Mrs Morris was probably the Armstrongs' housekeeper. She had that air of deference as she gave them a polite smile and left them standing in the hall.

'What are we doing here?' Rachel hissed, as soon as the woman was out of earshot. Mrs Morris had disappeared through a door at the far end of a panelled entrance hall, and although Rachel felt sure she had nothing to worry about, the house was amazingly quiet. Too quiet.

'Looking at the house,' said Ben innocently. 'Isn't that what I said?'

'The Armstrongs' house?'

'They own it, certainly,' Ben agreed, gesturing towards the door on their left. 'Shall we start here?'

Rachel looked horrified. 'You can't just wander round the house unescorted!'

'Why not?'

She gave him a retiring look.

'All right.' He sauntered across the carpeted floor and swung open the door into a cool sitting-room. 'When I said the Armstrongs own the house, they do. But they're not here right now.'

Rachel stared at him. 'Where are they?'

'Saudi Arabia.'

She thought she'd misheard him. 'Where?'

'Saudi Arabia,' he repeated carelessly. 'Stop worrying about the Armstrongs. Tell me what you think of this room?'

Rachel expelled her breath in a noisy gasp. 'You brought me here, knowing full well the Armstrongs wouldn't be at home!'

'Yes.' There was an edge of impatience to his voice now. 'We don't need the Armstrongs to show us round. We can do it perfectly well by ourselves.'

Rachel shook her head. 'Why should we—no, I'll re-phrase that—why should *I* want to look at a house I have no intention of seeing again?'

Ben stepped into the sitting-room, but his voice drifted back to her. 'I'm looking for a house in the district. I thought this was worth a look.'

CHAPTER NINE

'WHAT?'

Ben's reply brought her unwillingly—but swiftly—to the open doorway. And, in spite of the anger she was feeling, she couldn't help the involuntary gasp of admiration that escaped her at the sight of the room beyond. Although it had obviously been some time since anyone had bothered to redecorate, nothing could hide the simple beauty of its tall walls and high, corniced ceiling. It was a large room, almost square in shape, with an exquisite marble fireplace, presently filled with a huge vase of dried flowers. But Rachel could imagine how it would look when a fire was lit in the wide hearth, and the curtains drawn across two of the long windows she had seen earlier from the drive. At present they gave a panoramic view of the parkland, and the impression created was one of lightness and space.

'Beautiful, isn't it?' Ben said carelessly, standing in the middle of the worn Aubusson carpet, low-heeled boots set wide apart, hands tucked into the back pockets of his jeans. 'I knew you'd be impressed.'

Rachel gathered her objections about her. 'What did you mean? You're looking for a house in the district? You live in London.'

'Don't be obtuse,' responded Ben, abandoning his stance and walking towards her, and she backed hastily out of his way. 'I can own two houses, can't I?' His brows arched at her sudden withdrawal. 'Didn't I tell you it was for sale?'

'You know you didn't,' declared Rachel shortly, but she had already guessed. And she knew that Daisy would love it. Particularly, if she was allowed to get a horse of her own to ride in the grounds.

'Well, what do you think?' he asked now, opening another door to display a large, book-lined library, ideal as a study for someone working at home. Across the hall, a spacious dining-room opened into a Victorian-styled conservatory, with a paved patio beyond, suitable for summer barbecues.

'There's a pool-house, too,' he continued, gesturing through the octagonal windows of the conservatory. 'Though the pool's been drained all winter. It's heated, believe it or not, by solar panels in the roof of the pool-house. And there are screens to roll back if the weather's very hot.'

Rachel took a breath. 'Why are you telling me all this? Why have you brought me here?'

Ben shook his head. 'Humour me,' he replied indulgently. 'I wanted you to see it.' He glanced around the hall with a critical eye, and then gazed up the curving staircase. 'Come on. I'll show you the bedrooms.'

'No.' Rachel dug in her heels.

'Why not?'

She swallowed, determined not to let him see how he had disconcerted her. 'There's no point. And besides, Mrs Morris——'

'—will think it decidedly odd if you stay down here,' Ben finished for her. 'I noticed you didn't contradict me when I said you were my wife. Don't you think it's a little late to be having second thoughts?'

'I'm not having second thoughts.' Rachel could hear her voice rising and struggled to control it. 'I didn't contradict you when you said I was your wife because I didn't want to embarrass you. But you don't appreciate that. You don't care how you embarrass me.'

'By inviting you to look at the bedrooms?'

Put like that it did sound neurotic, but Rachel refused to be deterred. 'By bringing me here,' she declared, though they both knew she was lying. 'I'm not interested in the house, Ben. I'm not interested in you.'

'Then you've nothing to worry about, have you?' he commented drily, starting up the wide staircase. 'Unless you don't really mean it, of course.'

'In your eye,' muttered Rachel inaudibly, refusing to give him the satisfaction of a defensive response. But, as she watched him mount the stairs she knew she had to follow him. Not just to prove she meant what she said, but because it would be embarrassing if Mrs Morris decided to check on her guests.

The upper floor of the house was laid out much like the lower one, with each individual set of rooms opening from the central landing. There was a master suite, and a guest suite, each with its own dressing-room and bathroom, and three smaller apartments, with only dressing facilities, that shared the third bathroom.

'Of course, the dressing-rooms here could be converted to bathrooms, too,' Ben remarked, after considering the plumbing arrangements. 'But that's not an immediate necessity. How many bathrooms does one person need?' He returned to the master suite, and went to stand by the windows. With his hands pushed casually into his pockets again, he looked thoughtfully out at the parkland that stretched away from the front of the house. 'With some redecoration, I believe it could be habitable by late summer. Just in time to pick our own apples in the orchard, and light fires in those huge fireplaces downstairs.'

Rachel expelled her breath. 'You always did have a vivid imagination,' she said shortly.

'Why?' He turned to look at her now, and although she was standing safely by the door, with no possible chance of his cornering her in this place, she felt a twinge of alarm.

'Well—it's how you earn your living,' she said defensively. 'Besides, you've never picked an apple or lit a fire in your life.'

Ben lifted his shoulders. 'I can learn.'

It wasn't the answer she had expected, and she knew a momentary pang. But, 'I suppose so,' she conceded tautly, taking a steadying grasp of the handle. 'Well—can we go now?'

Ben shrugged. 'After we've seen the garden at the back. I believe there's a tree-house. According to the details they sent me about the house, it's been there since the Armstrongs' children were small.'

Preceding him down the stairs, Rachel could afford to be generous. 'And they're not small now?'

'No. They're all grown up and married—three of them, anyway. The second son is divorced, I believe. Some problem with the au pair.'

Rachel's head shot round. 'Is that supposed to be funny?'

'No.' But Ben's expression was unreadable. 'Here—we'll go this way,' he added, as they reached the hall again. 'We can go out through the conservatory. Mrs Morris knows what we're doing.'

'Does she?'

But Rachel's reply was only rhetorical. She was wishing she did; wishing she had a clearer notion of why Ben had brought her here. Oh, he was obviously interested in buying the house, and there was no denying that with the right interior designer, the results could be incredible. But she would never live here. This would never be her home.

Ben opened the conservatory door, and they stepped out on to the patio. Unlike the house, the garden had been well cared for and the borders were thick with flowering shrubs. Between clumps of azaleas, tulips and narcissus grew in wild profusion, and the westerly winds had brought primroses and wood anemones to cluster in sheltered beds. The blossom was out on the trees in the orchard: creamy white and palest pink, it scattered across the lawns like strewn confetti. The comparison wasn't appropriate, but the imagery was apt.

Rachel realised that, unlike the house, which needed a serious redecoration, the garden simply required a loving hand. And evidently someone cared enough to tend its lawns and flower beds. Without regular care, it would have quickly become rank and overgrown. As it was, it was a fitting setting for the house, whose mellowed walls seemed friendly in the dusky evening light.

'Can you walk across the grass?' Ben asked now, and because she was still bemused by the natural beauty of the setting Rachel didn't think before nodding. It was only as she followed him across the spongy lawn that she remembered she was eager to get away from here. But having committed herself, she was obliged to go on, through a gateway in the hedge, and into the blossoming orchard.

'Apples—pears—and these are plum trees,' announced Ben threading his way between the maze of trunks. 'There are cherry trees, as well——' he grimaced '—somewhere. And there's bushes of raspberries and blueberries in the vegetable garden. And a couple of greenhouses, which Mrs Morris's husband looks after. He's the gardener here, by the way. And her daughter helps out at dinner parties.' He grinned. 'It's sort of like a family concern. The Morrises have probably been here longer than the Armstrongs.'

Rachel kept her face straight with an effort. When he was being nice, the urge to respond to him was almost overpowering. It was with the utmost difficulty that she directed her gaze away from his lean, attractive features, and she wasn't aware of any danger until his hand came to rest on the bark of the tree beside her head.

She turned automatically, her shoulders coming up against the trunk behind her, and he moved to block her escape. His other arm made her his prisoner, and she realised how naïve she had been to think he was trustworthy.

'Don't you think this is rather silly?' she asked now, remembering her words had had more success than her

physical strength. All right, there had always been Daisy
or her mother in the background before. But for her to
attempt to fight with him here was obviously doomed
to failure.

'I agree,' he said, and for a moment she thought he
was agreeing with her. 'We shouldn't be fighting,
Rachel,' he added, and his lips curved in mocking intent.
'There are so many other, pleasurable things we could
do. Like this, for example.' He touched the honeycomb
of her ear with his tongue. 'I've always loved the taste
of your skin.'

Rachel breathed shallowly. 'Shouldn't that be a
woman's skin—*any* woman's skin?' she suggested
pointedly, hanging on to her composure for grim life.
'Elena's, for example. How did Elena's skin taste?
Sweeter, I suppose. Well, she was much younger.'

'I have no idea how Elena's skin tastes,' he replied, a
scowl briefly marring the dark beauty of his features.
'As I said then, and as I'll say again now, I never touched
Elena. I did offer to help her, however. Before she told
you all those lies, of course.'

'To help her!' Rachel was scornful. Then, realising
she was getting emotional again, she daringly took
another tack. 'What do you want, Ben?' she demanded.
'One last—screw—for old times' sake? Well, go ahead.
Why don't you do it? If that's what it takes to get you
off my back, I guess I can stand the inconvenience.'

Ben's lips tightened, and for a moment she thought
her ploy had worked. No man, she assured herself, not
even Ben, would want her on those terms. It had been
an inspired move to challenge his masculinity. It was obviously the last thing he'd expected, and she felt a momentary swirl of relief. But only momentary...

'You flatter me,' he said suddenly, silkily, and removing his hand from where it rested on the bark, he
stroked his knuckles down her cheek.

His hand was cold, but where it brushed her cheek it
left a trail of fire. Heat, hot and strong, surged into her

face at its passing, and the urge to twist away from him was practically uncontrollable.

But she stayed where she was, stiff and unresponsive, as he allowed his hand to trail along her jawline. She had to do this, she told herself, as his thumb brushed her lips and his finger touched the tender lobe of her ear. Unless she could convince him she meant what she said, she'd never be free.

'Do you mean it?' he asked softly, and Rachel's attempt to swallow almost choked her.

'I—yes. Of course I mean it,' she got out at last, even though this was not going quite the way she'd imagined. Some other insult was called for, and she struggled to find the words. 'If you're so desperate for someone to have sex with.'

'Right.' Ben's mouth flattened. 'Unbutton your blouse.'

Rachel gagged. 'I beg your——'

'I said, unbutton your blouse.'

'I know what you said, damn you.' Rachel pushed her shoulders back against the hard wood. 'But—you don't mean it.'

Ben's eyes narrowed. 'You said you did,' he reminded her, and her knees went weak.

'I know, but——'

Rachel broke off abruptly. Of course, she thought fiercely, this was just another attempt to provoke her. He didn't really intend going through with it. Particularly not here, in the Armstrongs' orchard.

Moistening her lips, she started again. 'I didn't imagine you meant here,' she declared, proud that there was practically no tremor in her voice, in spite of her inward panic.

'Where, then?' For a moment she couldn't think what he meant. 'Your house? I doubt your mother would approve. My hotel? Aren't you afraid your farmer might find out?'

Rachel managed to get the saliva past the constriction in her throat. 'Somewhere else,' she said wildly, already planning never to let herself get into such a position again. She wasn't as dispassionate as she'd thought. And she certainly doubted her ability to convince him.

'Not possible,' he intoned, running one finger under the collar of her blouse, and somehow managing to dislodge the top button. 'Open your blouse, Rachel. We haven't got all night. Much as the knowledge pains me, there's a limit to how long we can comfortably stay in the garden.'

'Before Mrs Morris comes looking for us, you mean?' Rachel asked eagerly, wondering what her chances were of distracting him for a while.

'Before we get chilled to the bone,' Ben amended smoothly. 'Come on. What are you waiting for? I can see you still wear a bra.'

Rachel caught her breath. 'You bastard!'

'Hey.' Ben looked aggrieved. 'You started this. You can't blame me now because I'm taking you up on it.'

Rachel gazed at him with glittering eyes. 'You don't really want to do this.'

'Oh, but I do.' He was infuriatingly intent. 'How was it you put it? One last—well—for old times' sake? Yes. That seems fair. I like it.' He took one of her cold hands and brought it resistingly to his lips. 'Don't keep me waiting. I may decide that once is not enough.'

'I won't do it.' Rachel pulled her hand out of his grasp and pressed it against her midriff.

'Oh, you will,' he informed her softly. 'It seems like the only way I can get to you. You don't want to talk, and you won't listen. So I'm driven to other methods.'

'I'll talk.'

'Too late.'

'I'll listen then.'

'Oh, Rachel, stop prevaricating. We both know you're only stalling. You don't mean a word you say.'

'I do——'

'Do it, Rachel. Don't make me do it for you. I may just decide to rip the buttons off, and how would you explain that to Mrs Morris?'

'You—pig!' Rachel's trembling fingers sought the placket of her blouse, and she slowly removed the buttons from their holes. 'I'll never forgive you for this. Never!'

'Then I'll just have to live with that, won't I?' he essayed huskily. 'Oh, Rachel' He drew an uneven breath as the creamy mounds of her upper breasts were revealed. 'Unfasten the bra. Then let me look.'

Rachel reached behind her, under her jacket and the now loosened blouse, and unhooked the bra. Her fingers were shaking so much, it took her several attempts to do it, and by the time she'd succeeded Ben's hands were already peeling the white cotton out of the way.

Then, with almost reverential care, he cupped the two globes in his hands, weighing them with evident satisfaction, rubbing his thumbs across the treacherously swollen tips.

'Beautiful,' he said thickly, transferring his gaze to her flushed face, and Rachel wondered how long her legs would continue to support her. His abrasive thumbs were causing more than just a tingling in her upper body. Deep in her stomach, a smouldering ember of awareness was threatening to burst into flame.

'Do you like this?' he asked, brushing his lips against hers, before bending his head to take one straining nipple into his mouth. He laved the sensitive peak with his tongue, and then sucked on it strongly, causing that curl of awareness to shoot down to her toes.

'I—no,' she got out hoarsely, but she knew he knew she was lying. Already her hands itched to slide into his hair and bring his head closer to her body. Already her lips were parting, anticipating the wet invasion of his tongue.

'Undress me,' he said, lifting his head from her breasts, his lips moist from his hungry possession, and the resistance drained out of her. With his eyes on hers he brought her hands to his chest, and, although she'd sworn to herself she wouldn't do this, her fingers fumbled to obey him.

Jerking her eyes from his, she tried to concentrate on what her hands were doing to the exclusion of all else, but her gaze was instinctively drawn to the taut fabric of his trousers. His manhood thrust against his zip, and she hadn't even tried to arouse him, she thought unsteadily. Dear God, what was she doing? She couldn't allow this to go on.

But the urge to touch him was growing stronger, and she dragged her eyes away before she gave in to the temptation. His unbuttoned shirt revealed his flat stomach, and the arrowing of hair that thickened below his navel. She remembered that distinctly—without the unmistakable evidence of his sex.

Ben moved closer when his shirt was unfastened, and his fine chest hair was absurdly sensuous against the tender swell of her breasts. He rubbed himself against her, until the needs he was arousing threatened to overwhelm her, and then jammed his thigh between her legs as his mouth came down on hers.

His kiss was hard, yet soft, aggressive, yet amazingly sensual, drawing a response from her she was incapable of holding back. With her skirt rucked up above her knees, and his thigh riding against the sensitive heart of her femininity she was powerless to resist him. His tongue in her mouth was playing a tantalising game of advance and retreat, and the fists she'd balled against his chest slid helplessly about his neck.

Everything was tactile, from the heat his thigh was generating, to the virile softness of his hair. Its silky strands wound themselves about her fingers, and she abandoned any hope of deliverance. Digging her nails into his scalp, she held his lips to hers, opening her mouth wide to the power of his possession.

'You do like it,' he whispered tormentingly, when the need for air forced him to pant unsteadily into the hollow of her shoulder. 'Oh, God, do you have any idea what you're doing to me?'

Rachel thought perhaps she did, if it was anything like what his mouth and hands and leg were doing to her. And when she felt his hand against the back of her thigh, pushing her skirt even higher, she was fairly positive.

'Suspenders,' he said unsteadily, not without some satisfaction, when he discovered the bare skin her stocking-tops exposed. His fingers moved possessively to the moist junction of her thighs, and he uttered a shaky laugh. 'Oh, God, baby, you're ready for me. Your panties are wet!'

She should have been embarrassed, but she wasn't. When his fingers slid into the moist cleft he had prepared for them, she couldn't stop herself from arching against him. Sensation, like an ever-expanding circle, was spreading out from that sensitive core. When he rubbed his fingers against the slick nub, the excitement was all-enveloping, and when he lifted her leg and wrapped it around him, her senses swam dizzily to the edge.

'One minute, just one minute,' he muttered unevenly, his own fingers fumbling now as he sought to release his belt. The buckle jammed and he swore softly, but eventually he succeeded in his task.

'Let me,' said Rachel, in a voice she hardly recognised as her own. Brushing his hands aside, she eased the zip carefully down its length, and then caught her breath convulsively when his sex spilled into her hands.

'No underwear,' she said almost matter-of-factly, but Ben only pressed himself against her.

'No time,' he said unsteadily, delivering hot, drugging kisses to her mouth. 'You do it,' he added, tearing her panties in his haste to get inside her, and with infinite care, she brought him to her sheath.

Amazingly, it was like the first time they ever made love. Three years since the separation—and much longer than that since Ben had possessed her body as well as her soul—his invasion was initially that: an invasion. She was still tense, in spite of her body's readiness for him, and when Ben eased his way inside her he sensed her instinctive resistance.

But it didn't last. Their need for one another was overwhelming, and when he crushed her back against the trunk of the tree behind her, she wrapped both legs about him.

And it was good, so good. Fast, and hot, and sensual, but so wonderfully satisfying that Rachel couldn't help the breathless cries that sprang from her lips. He was big and strong, powerfully muscled, but so smoothly formed that his skin slid slickly into hers. And he filled her completely, stretching the space that had been empty for so long, causing her muscles to expand, then clench tightly around him.

He tried to be gentle, but it wasn't enough, and pretty soon he was thrusting heavily against her. And she didn't care. She welcomed his hunger. She was hungry, too. And in any case, her senses were already spinning far beyond her control.

It was soon over. The shuddering, shattering climax that enveloped her was matched by Ben's own groan of release. She felt his seed, felt its warmth spreading inside her, and the after-shocks of his lovemaking lingered sweetly in her bones . . .

CHAPTER TEN

RACHEL lay in bed, staring at the ceiling. She had been lying there for the better part of three hours, and she was no nearer going to sleep now than she had been when she climbed between the sheets.

But how was she supposed to sleep? she wondered bitterly. How was she supposed to relax, when all she could think about was what she had done that afternoon? She wasn't naturally a deceiver, and it sat badly with her that she had had to lie to Simon that evening. But if she'd told him what had happened he'd never have forgiven her.

And who would blame him? she thought unhappily. Being unfaithful to the man you loved was just as damning, even if the man you had cheated with was technically still your husband. And, no matter how she tried to wriggle out of it, she had been as much to blame for Ben's behaviour as he was. She'd invited him to do it. Whatever defensive motives she might attribute to the suggestion, she had put the idea in Ben's head.

Of course, it had probably been there already. She knew that. But without her co-operation it might never have been put into action. It didn't matter that her intentions had been good, or that she'd never really believed he'd take her up on it. He had. And what was worse, she'd actively encouraged him to do it.

Which was the real crux of the matter, she acknowledged, punching her pillow hard before turning on to her side. If Ben had taken advantage of her in the truest sense, she wouldn't be lying here now, feeling as guilty as a rattlesnake. If he'd forced her to have sex with him, she might, she just might, have been able to justify her behaviour.

125

But he hadn't. Not really. Oh, he'd made her unbutton her blouse and her bra, and at that moment she
had wanted to crucify him. But, after he touched her,
after he bent his head and kissed her breasts, the will to
resist him had left her.

A shiver slid down her spine at the memory, and in
spite of herself her fingers sought the sensitive tips of
her breasts. They were still tender, and if she'd allowed
Simon the same sexual freedom she'd allowed Ben he'd
have seen it for himself. Her nipples were red and sore,
and there were marks from Ben's evening stubble on her
skin.

Bruises on her thighs, too, where he had gripped the
tops of her legs as he drove himself into her. Her hand
strayed lower, finding the muscles that still protested at
the invasion. Between her legs, a pulse was racing,
matching the rapid beating of her heart.

She allowed her breath to escape in a shuddering sigh.
Lord, what was she doing, lying here, thinking about a
man who had probably betrayed her time and time again.
Ben was just the same. He had always been good. The
trouble was, she wasn't the only woman to know it...

He was probably gloating now, lying in bed—if he
was in his own bed at the hotel—enjoying the satisfaction of knowing he had called her bluff. He must have
known she'd lost control, known the moment when
studied resistance became active participation. However
determined she had been to show him she found his advances distasteful, ultimately he'd had the final victory.
It was she who'd cried aloud at the sensations she was
feeling, she who'd wept in silence at the beauty they had
lost.

Not that he'd said a lot as they walked back to the
house. When she'd been expecting him to glory in her
defeat, he'd made no reference at all to what had gone
before. After adjusting his own clothes, he'd waited with
his back turned for her to do the same. Then, they had
walked back to the conservatory, just as if all they'd

been doing was exploring the grounds. He'd been polite to Mrs Morris, and subdued on the journey home. And although Daisy had come dancing out to see him he'd refused her invitation to come in.

Of course, Rachel had been grateful for his silence. Even if she was somewhat puzzled by his restraint. It might have been easier if he had said or done something to arouse her anger, she reflected now. She badly wanted to hate him, but as it was she just hated herself.

She rolled on to her back. But what of it? she asked herself impatiently. What was she making such a fuss about? Dear God, all he'd done was have sex with her. If she'd been a little more generous with Simon, she might have found a better way to forget.

But she couldn't have made love with Simon tonight, she assured herself grimly. Apart from anything else, they had spent the evening with her mother. Mrs Collins had insisted that if Rachel and Simon did intend to live together, she should get to know him better. A circumstance, Rachel couldn't help suspecting, that owed more to the anxiety she'd seen in her daughter's face when Ben brought her home than to any real desire to make amends.

And, typically, Simon had chosen to be unusually tolerant that evening. He had parried every criticism levelled against him with a jovial smile. He seemed determined to show Mrs Collins that he had a sense of humour, and Rachel felt even worse because she couldn't respond.

'Has Rachel told you, she and Daisy are coming to live in one of my cottages, until we can get married?' he asked, catching her as she passed his chair, and pulling her down on to the arm. It enabled him to slip his arm about her, and, although Rachel had wanted to escape, her conscience kept her where she was.

'I understand the matter's under discussion,' Mrs Collins had responded pleasantly, but the look she had exchanged with her daughter was anything but. 'I fear

Rachel's husband may have some objections,' she added. 'After all, it will be less convenient for Daisy to catch her bus.'

Simon visibly squashed the retort he'd planned, and forced a polite smile. 'Ah, but Daisy won't need to catch a bus, when she starts at the school in Lower Morton. It's the school I went to, and my father before me. If it's good enough for us, I'm sure it's good enough for Daisy.'

'If she wanted to be a farmer,' murmured Mrs Collins, under her breath, and Rachel, who had heard her, cast her a warning glance. 'Well, I doubt *her* father will agree with you,' she finished pointedly. 'And nor, I suspect, will Daisy. She's happy at Lady's Mount.'

Simon's smile thinned. 'I do think this is a matter for Rachel and me to decide,' he said, his arm around his fiancée's hips tightening possessively. He paused. 'I understand you're going to live in New Zealand, Mrs Collins. I'm sure Daisy will want to go and stay with you. It'll be easier if school fees aren't involved.'

Rachel could sit still no longer. 'Does anyone want a cup of coffee,' she asked, 'before I go and settle Daisy down for the night. The programme she wanted to see should be over by now, but if I don't turn the television off she'll watch it all night!'

'She has a television in her bedroom?'

Simon sounded scandalised, and Rachel exchanged another defensive look with her mother, before saying swiftly, 'It's easier that way. Besides, all her friends have one. And it means we can both watch the programmes we like. I don't care for the repeats of shows like *Happy Days* and *Mork and Mindy*, and she certainly doesn't want to watch the news.'

'Then perhaps she should,' declared Simon, without thinking. Then, as if realising he was being too heavy, he leavened his words with a little humour. 'After all, these are the kids who are going to be our future politicians! I doubt if *Mork and Mindy* have an opinion on the economy.'

'No.'

Rachel decided not to elaborate, but as she repeated her question about having coffee she was aware of the tension in the room.

'I'd like a gin and tonic instead,' said her mother, as if desperate for a stimulant. 'Perhaps Mr Barrass would like one, too. We don't want to be up all night.'

'Simon, call me Simon, please,' he exclaimed, and then looking up at Rachel, he shook his head. 'Coffee's fine with me, darling,' he assured her. 'Unlike your mother, I never have a problem going to sleep.'

'I'm not surprised,' remarked Mrs Collins, in another aside only her daughter could hear, and after turning on the coffee-maker Rachel went wearily upstairs. No matter what he did, Simon was never going to win her mother over. And she, herself, was too tired tonight to continue playing pig-in-the-middle.

Which was ironic, she thought now, turning on to her back again. Because she had felt tired earlier. But that kind of tiredness didn't last. Not when it was her mind that was keeping her awake.

'You're not really going to take Daisy away from Lady's Mount, are you?' her mother asked the next morning, after the little girl had left to catch her bus. 'I think it would be a mistake, I really do.'

'I haven't decided,' said Rachel shortly, dumping their empty coffee-cups on the drainer. 'Um—will you need the car today? If so, I'd better get going.'

Mrs Collins frowned. 'I don't think so. I had a lovely day in Cheltenham yesterday. Which reminds me, you still haven't told me where Ben took you. With Daisy all ears, I didn't like to ask. And then with your farmer friend coming last night, I didn't get the chance.'

Rachel got her tone even with some difficulty. 'Don't you think you could call him Simon, Mother? I know you don't like him, but you could at least use his name.'

Mrs Collins sighed. 'Very well. I'll try and remember.' She paused. 'So—where did you go?'

'With Ben?' Rachel could be obtuse, too.

'Of course with Ben.' Her mother looked a little tight-lipped now. 'I assume you're angry with me for not warning you. Well, I did think about it, but I knew what you would say.'

'Damn right!' Rachel couldn't disguise her resentment now, and she wondered how blasé her mother would be if she knew Ben had made love to her.

Not that what had happened between them could be graced by such a euphemistic description. They had had sex, pure and simple. However gratifying—however satisfying—it had been, she had no illusions about the outcome. She could only hope he didn't intend to use what had happened as a means of manipulation. What would she do if he threatened to tell Simon?

'There's no need to swear.' Her mother sniffed. 'Perhaps I should have told you, but Ben was so mysterious when he rang that I didn't think it was fair to spoil his surprise.'

His surprise!

'But, if you don't want to tell me about it, I shall quite understand.' She pursed her lips. 'Even if, whatever your objections, you were obviously in no hurry to get back. You two were absent for the better part of two hours! If I didn't know better, I'd wonder if you didn't have something to hide!'

Rachel braced herself against the sink. 'And what if I have?' she demanded recklessly, and then wished she hadn't when she saw her mother's stunned expression.

'Rachel!'

'Oh, I'm not serious.' Rachel bent her head and turned away, pretending to be searching for a tissue in her bag. 'If you must know,' she was obliged to be honest now, 'he wanted to show me a house, that's all. Some manor house over at Watersmeet. He says he's thinking of buying it.'

'A house!' Mrs Collins blinked. 'Good heavens! Do you think he's moving back to the district?'

'Who knows?' Rachel felt weary. 'In any case, it's nothing to do with me. Or you either, for that matter.'

'So why did he take you to see it?' She should have known her mother wouldn't let it rest there. 'What's it like? Is it old? Did you meet the owners? Did he say you were his wife?'

'It's unoccupied,' said Rachel flatly. 'Apart from the housekeeper, that is. And I don't know why he took me to see it. Unless he wanted to prove he could provide a better home for Daisy than I could.'

'Ben's not like that.' Mrs Collins looked thoughtful. 'It must have been a big house, if it took you over an hour to go round it.'

Rachel felt a faint trace of colour enter her cheeks at her mother's words, and expelling an unsteady breath, she made for the door. 'Yes, it was,' she said shortly, gathering up her jacket. 'I'll see you about half-past twelve. I'll bring some sausage rolls for our lunch.'

Simon picked her up at seven that evening. As her mother had agreed to babysit, he was taking her over to Kingsmead, to see the cottage he had told her about.

'It's not big,' he said, as the Range Rover bounced up the track to the farm. 'But it is cosy. And there are two bedrooms, as well as a bathroom. Septic tank drainage, of course, but that's not a problem. And solid fuel central heating. Not something you usually find in cottages.'

'Solid fuel?' Rachel grimaced. 'I've never had to light a boiler before.'

'Oh, you'll soon get used to it.' Simon smiled. 'And I'll be on hand in emergencies.'

Rachel nodded. 'Well, I don't suppose there'll be too many of those,' she averred optimistically. 'After all, if Ben's agreeable, the divorce might be final by Christmas. Then, after we're married, we won't need the cottage, will we? We'll be sharing the farmhouse with you.'

'Yes.' But Simon didn't sound entirely convinced. 'Well, that's something I wanted to talk to you about, actually. Mother's not very keen on sharing her kitchen with another woman. She'd been mistress here so long, she regards the place as hers.'

Rachel's stomach hollowed. 'So you want us to start our married life in the cottage.'

'Of course not.' But Simon's face had reddened anyway. 'That's what I wanted to talk to you about. I'm thinking of building a second house for us. Still on the farm, of course, but some distance from the main building.'

'I see.'

'It's a good idea.' Simon was quick to seize the initiative. 'I mean—our very own home. And modern, too. Not like Kingsmead, which even I have to admit needs some updating.'

Rachel licked her lips. 'And how long do you think it will take to build this second house?'

'A few months.' Simon was vague. 'I'll have to apply for planning permission, of course, and I'll need an architect to draw up the plans. We could plan it together. You and me—and Daisy, too, of course. Don't look like that. You must have known my mother wouldn't take too kindly to having a child about the house. She's too old...'

And too possessive, though Rachel tensely, remembering what her mother had said about Mrs Barrass not wanting to relinquish her role as mistress of the house. She refused to contemplate the possibility that the rest of what she had said might be true, too. Simon did want to marry her. He did! He was just considering his mother's feelings, that was all. An admirable trait, surely.

The cottage was approached along a track made muddy by the spell of wet weather. It stood, remote and unadorned, at the corner of the north field, with little in the way of protection from the prevailing westerly winds.

Inside, it was a little more prepossessing. As Simon had said, it had two bedrooms, both of a decent size, and a big old-fashioned bathroom. Downstairs, there was a large room that served as both a dining and living area, and a kitchen that was fairly basic, but which sported a modern electric cooker. The heating, both for the water and the old iron radiators, was provided by the fire in the living-room. A disadvantage in hot weather, Rachel reflected, but not a problem at this time of year.

'Well? What do you think?'

Simon evidently expected her approval as he stood in the larger of the two bedrooms, surveying his surroundings with undisguised enthusiasm. The fact that the room was still furnished with the previous tenant's four-poster, and smelled a little musty, didn't seem to bother him. Or the fact that there were lighter squares on the walls, where pictures or framed photographs, had been removed.

'It needs—redecorating,' said Rachel at last, choosing the least controversial reply, and Simon snorted.

'Well, of course it does,' he exclaimed. 'But what does a bit of paint and paper cost? So long as the walls are solid and the roof doesn't leak...' He shrugged. 'I mean, it's not bad, is it?'

Privately, Rachel thought it was awful. Not because of its size, but because of where it was. Stuck out here, miles from anywhere, with a track that was probably impassable in the bad weather. What if there was an emergency? What if Daisy was ill? If her car was laid up she'd be helpless.

'I'm—not sure,' she said now, moving to the window, and looking out on the water-logged garden. Evidently the drainage left much to be desired, too, and she wondered if the musty smell was dampness.

Simon came up behind her, sliding his arms around her waist, and propping his chin on her shoulder. 'Come on,' he said. 'It's only for a few months. And it means we can be together. Isn't that what we both want?'

Rachel stiffened. 'What do you mean—together?' she asked, restraining the impulse to pull away from him. Right at this moment, any kind of physical contact was an anathema to her, and she closed her eyes convulsively when he turned his lips against her neck.

'What do you think I mean?' he countered softly, his breath moist against her ear. 'This will be our very own love-nest, with no one to interrupt us, or tell us what to do.'

'No!' That was too much, and uncaring of what he might think of her actions, Rachel twisted out of his arms. 'That is—I don't want myself—or Daisy—causing any more gossip around here.'

Simon scowled. 'I suppose I have your mother to thank for this.'

'No...'

'Well, you were perfectly willing to accept my offer before she came on the scene.' His lips curled. 'And we mustn't forget your husband, must we? I bet he's put his oar in, as well.'

'It's not like that.'

'Then what is it like? What's changed your mind?'

Rachel sighed. 'Simon, when you first mentioned the idea of us moving into one of the cottages, it was on the understanding that when my divorce was final we'd get married.'

'And so we will.'

'But when?' Rachel spread her hands. 'You say you're not prepared to start our married life here. So are we supposed to put our wedding off indefinitely? Until some nameless planner decides that you can lay the foundations of the other house?'

Simon pushed his hands into the pockets of his hacking jacket, and rocked back and forwards on his heels. 'I didn't realise you were so desperate to get another ring on your finger,' he said unpleasantly. 'What does it matter how long we wait, so long as we get there eventually?'

'It matters,' said Rachel evenly, taking a backward step. 'And, if it's all the same to you, I think Daisy and I will stay where we are until we can get married. OK?'

'No, it's not OK.' Simon was angry. 'I've made special arrangements so you can have this place. One of my workers is getting married, and he asked me if he and his wife could move in here. I told him no, and ran the risk of losing him. Good cowmen are hard to find these days, and Billy Elliot is one of the best.'

'Well, now you can tell him he can have it, after all,' returned Rachel tightly, feeling the first twinges of a headache needling at her temples. She took a steadying breath and glanced towards the door. 'Are we going to call and see your mother?' she asked, determined not to let what had happened upset her. The last person she wanted to see at this moment was Mrs Barrass, but somehow she had to heal the breach, and losing her temper too would accomplish nothing.

Simon's mouth compressed for a moment, but then, as if realising he was being boorish, his expression softened. 'In a minute,' he said, coming towards her, and grasping her upper arms. 'We're not in any hurry.' He drew her towards him, his hungry eyes running possessively over her pale face. 'I'm sorry,' he added, bending his head to kiss her. 'I didn't intend for us to fall out over this. Am I forgiven?'

Rachel steeled herself not to turn her face away from his lips, wondering why she was suddenly so averse to his affections. It was his attitude, she told herself. The selfish way he had intended to ride roughshod over her feelings. Just because he had apologised, it didn't mean it could be forgotten.

'So,' she said, keeping her voice steady with an effort, 'you understand how I feel?'

'I understand I haven't gone about this in the right way,' he amended softly, his hands sliding down her spine. 'I think you need a little more time to adjust to the idea. Now——' his hands settled heavily on her hips '—stop wasting time and kiss me. I have a notion to christen this old bed.'

'No!'

Rachel was horrified, as much by her revulsion at the thought of letting Simon make love to her as by the idea of lying down on the musty bedspread. And it showed.

'What do you mean, no?' Simon was exasperated. 'Rachel, don't you think this has gone on long enough? All right, so you had a bad experience, and it's taken some time for you to get over it. But, I'm a man, for God's sake, not a boy. You can't put me off indefinitely. You've got to come to terms with the fact that all men are not alike.'

They certainly weren't, and Rachel was beginning to wonder what kind of a judge of men she really was. 'Look,' she said, pressing her hands against his chest, 'it'll be different when we're married——'

'When we're married?' Simon gave a scornful laugh. 'We may never get married at this rate. For heaven's sake, woman, you can't honestly expect us to wait until we're married to consummate this relationship. You knew what I had in mind when I first mentioned the cottage. Somewhere private, where we could be alone.'

'No.'

Despite his resistance, Rachel managed to extricate herself from his embrace. She was unwillingly aware of the layer of fat that coated his chest and midriff as she forced herself away. Aware too, that she was making comparisons, when no comparison should be necessary.

She had been half afraid he might make something unpleasant of the encounter, but to her relief he merely brushed past her and started down the stairs. 'All right, let's go,' he muttered irritably, the red skin above his collar at the back evidence of his frustration. 'I told Mother we wouldn't be much above half an hour. I don't want her worrying that all's not as it should be.'

Which was probably why he'd been so amenable, thought Rachel weakly, never imagining she'd ever have reason to feel grateful to Mrs Barrass for anything. But obviously Simon didn't want her making any awkward accusations in his mother's hearing.

Simon locked the door, and they climbed back into the Range Rover for the bumpy ride back to the main house. Although the evening had been sunny when they set out, the sky was overcast now and rain spattered the windscreen. A fair approximation of her mood, thought Rachel ruefully, wondering why she suddenly felt so empty inside.

Mrs Barrass had obviously been expecting them. She opened the door as the Range Rover stopped, allowing a couple of collies to escape and jump about Rachel's ankles. A small woman, grey-haired, and stocky, like her son, she seemed to enjoy watching the younger woman trying to avoid the dogs' muddy paws.

'They won't hurt you,' she said scornfully. Then, to her son, 'You've been long enough. The tea's brewed and waiting.'

'Sorry, Mother.' Simon's smile, and the considerate way he drew back to let Rachel precede him into the house almost made her doubt her interpretation of his attitude at the cottage. But his eyes, meeting hers, still mirrored a cold defiance, and Rachel shivered as she stepped past him into the kitchen of Kingsmead.

'Did you like the cottage?'

Realising Mrs Barrass was speaking to her, Rachel sought a suitable reply. 'It's a little remote,' she said carefully, glancing about her at the heavy wooden dressers and massive leaded hearth. Perhaps she should be grateful Simon wasn't expecting her to live here, she thought, with a wry grimace. She could just imagine Mrs Barrass standing over her as she cleaned the grate.

'Remote?'

The older woman looked at her son, and Simon gave a careless shrug. 'I don't think Rachel's had time to consider all the advantages yet, Mother,' he said. 'Did you mention a cup of tea?'

Mrs Barrass gestured towards the pot, set on its stand on a table that had been scrubbed almost white. 'Seems to me she doesn't know how lucky she is to have a friend like you,' she declared, adding milk, willy-nilly, to the cups. Rachel felt like saying she didn't take milk, just to be awkward. She didn't like being spoken about, as if she wasn't there.

'Yes, well...' Simon glanced her way, and, as if realising he was in danger of losing any credibility he had, he made an attempt to rescue the situation. 'Rachel isn't used to living on a farm.'

'Then maybe you ought to think again before letting her move into the cottage,' retorted his mother shortly. 'I never did think it was a good idea. Cottages are for workers, not for bits of skirt!'

Rachel gasped. 'I beg your pardon——'

'You heard what I——'

'Yes, I did. And I want to know what you meant by it.'

'Mother! Rachel!'

Simon dived into the fray, red-faced and flustered at this turn of events, and Rachel, looking at him, began to wonder what he had said about her. The question had never come up before, and she supposed she had been guilty of thinking it was all a foregone conclusion. Surely he had told his mother he had asked her to marry him. Or, because she was still technically married, had he let her think it was something else?

'Don't—don't speak about Rachel like that, Mother,' Simon muttered now, albeit in a wheedling tone. 'She didn't ask to move into the cottage. I suggested it. As we—as we're walking out together, it seemed the least I could do.'

Rachel blinked. 'Simon, didn't you——?'

'I don't care whose idea it was,' declared Mrs Barrass, overriding Rachel's attempt to discover the truth. She looked at the other woman with a definite gleam of malice in her eyes. 'And don't think I don't know what you're up to, missy. Getting our Simon to support you! He's a generous soul, I know, but I won't stand by and let him be made a fool of.'

Rachel could hardly speak, she was so indignant. 'Whatever gave you the idea that I might make a fool of your son?' she demanded, when she could get her tongue round the words. 'And whatever you may think, he will not be supporting me, wherever I decide to live. I have a perfectly good job, and I can support myself, thank you. Whatever he's told you, I can do without his help.'

'Rachel——'

Simon groaned, but his mother took no notice of her son's dismay. 'Then why are you even looking at the cottage, if that husband of yours isn't threatening you with eviction? According to what Simon says, he's given you an ultimatum. He wants a divorce, or some such thing, and he intends to sell the house out from under you.'

Rachel was stunned. 'Is that what Simon told you?'

'Isn't it true?'

'No——'

'Mother, I never said any such thing!' Simon glared at Mrs Barrass now, and for a moment Rachel thought how absurdly alike they looked. 'What I said was, Rachel wants a divorce just as much as her husband. And—as the house belongs to her husband, she's looking for somewhere else to live.'

CHAPTER ELEVEN

'YOU were back fairly early last night, weren't you?' asked Mrs Collins at breakfast, and Rachel wondered how long she could go on without telling her mother what had happened. 'I was reading when you came in, and I was sure you'd see my light. I thought you might have come in and told me what the cottage is like. I didn't hear Simon's voice, so I assumed you were alone.'

'I was.' In all honesty, Rachel could have come in even sooner, but after Simon had dropped her off she'd sat for over an hour in the greenhouse. 'I didn't want to disturb you,' she added, not altogether truthfully. 'Gosh, is that the time? I really should get moving.'

'Rachel.' Her mother's voice arrested her, as she got up from the table. 'What's wrong? I know there's something. Can't you tell me?'

Rachel sighed. 'Oh, Simon and I have had a—a difference of opinion.'

Mrs Collins frowned. 'I'd say that was an occupational hazard as far as that man is concerned.'

'Yes, well—maybe it is.' Rachel hoped she might get away with the equivocation. 'Did—er—did you have a nice evening? Daisy wasn't any trouble, was she? She's so much enjoying having you here.'

'She's enjoying having her father here better,' remarked Mrs Collins, without rancour. She paused. 'Rachel, are you going to tell me what's troubling you? Or must I spend the day worrying that you'll have no one to confide in after I've gone.'

Rachel looked dismayed. 'You're leaving?'

'Tomorrow or the next day,' her mother confirmed gently. 'Rachel, I can't stay here indefinitely. I've told

140

Ralph I'll be back in New Zealand before the end of August, and there's such a lot to do.'

'Oh, yes.' Rachel felt hollow. 'Ralph.' He was the man her mother was going to marry. 'It seems so short a time, when you say it like that. I'll come and help you pack, of course. But I suppose there's quite a lot of sorting out to do.'

'That's right.' Mrs Collins caught her lower lip between her teeth. 'You could come with me, of course.'

'Tomorrow? Oh, I don't see how I——'

'I mean—to New Zealand,' corrected her mother firmly. 'You could. Ralph's a widower, as I've told you, and he has no children. In addition to which, he has this big house overlooking Auckland harbour. Daisy would love it, I'm sure.'

Rachel felt the unwelcome prick of tears behind her eyes. 'Oh, Mum, you know I can't do that.'

'Why not?'

'Well—because——'

'Because of Simon Barrass, I suppose.'

'Not exactly.'

'What do you mean, not exactly?' Her mother looked impatient. 'Something *has* happened, hasn't it? It wasn't just a difference of opinion you two had last night. What happened?' She looked anxious. 'He didn't—assault you or anything, did he? If he did, I'll——'

'Of course he didn't try to assault me.'

Rachel managed to sound almost amused at the suggestion, although the argument she had had with Simon on the way home had bordered on the physical at times. He had been furious with her for refusing to listen to what he saw as reason, and it had only been his fear of what more she might say to his mother, she was sure, that had forced him to control his temper.

And, maybe, an unwillingness to accept that their relationship had been fatally damaged, she conceded now. Simon was nothing if not a survivor, and she was sure he thought she would come round, once she had had time to think it over.

'So, what did happen?' persisted Mrs Collins. 'Was the cottage an absolute wash-out, or what?'

'It was—all right,' said Rachel cautiously. 'But, if you must know, Simon hadn't told his mother we were getting married.' She sighed. 'He may have been hoping to break the news to her gently. We'll never know. She got me angry, and I'm afraid I wasn't so discreet.'

'You told her?' Mrs Collins looked impressed.

'In a manner of speaking.' Rachel had no wish to go into the details. 'Um—I really do have to go, Mum. Mr Caldwell's just looking for an excuse to bawl me out.'

'Oh, very well.'

Her mother had no choice but to let her go, though Rachel guessed she hadn't heard the last of it so far as Mrs Collins was concerned. Her main hope was that she could avoid telling her the full extent of her disillusionment. After what had happened last night, she didn't see how she and Simon could ever share a life.

But that wasn't her mother's problem, and Rachel couldn't allow her to make it so. However appealing her offer might sound—and the idea of leaving England and escaping from the mess she had made of her life was tempting—she couldn't do it. This was her mother's time, not hers. All Mrs Collins should have on her mind at the moment was her own wedding. She shouldn't have to think about sharing her new home with her daughter and granddaughter. And, no matter how understanding Ralph was, Rachel doubted he'd appreciate having a ready-made family dumped on him before he'd even been on his honeymoon.

So, until her mother left England, she must try and maintain the fiction that she and Simon were still together. It shouldn't be too difficult, if Mrs Collins was leaving to go back to London soon. Besides, she had no desire for Ben to find out what had happened. After his behaviour, there was always the chance he'd think he was the reason she was having second thoughts.

Which wasn't true, she assured herself, despising the shiver of anticipation she felt just thinking about that scene in the orchard. God, how could she be so hypocritical as to despise Simon for lying to her? Was she any better, letting Ben do what he'd done?

And wasn't it also possible that it was Ben's treatment of her that had made her so wary of Simon? If she hadn't had the memory of that passionate interlude to distort her relationship with Simon, would she have reacted so negatively to his demands? She'd never know. And there was no denying the fact that he had kept the truth—if it was the truth—from his mother. His excuse had been that Mrs Barrass was old-fashioned; that until Rachel had got her divorce and was free, his mother couldn't regard her as his fiancée. There might be some truth in that, Rachel was prepared to accept, but nothing could alter the fact that he hadn't told her what he was doing.

The trouble was that since Ben had turned up, she had found it incredibly difficult to think positively about her future. She might not want to admit it, but he had destroyed her peace of mind, and although she didn't believe that she still loved him, the feelings he inspired in her were disruptively intense.

'I saw you and your husband going off together the other evening,' Cyril remarked, as they shared their coffee-break that morning. He had been off the previous day, but he had obviously been waiting to mention it. 'Does Barrass know you're still running around with Ben? I wouldn't have thought he'd be too keen.'

Rachel shrugged, refusing to be provoked. 'Ben gave me a lift home, that's all,' she said casually. 'I like that Meissen flower seller. Who'd have thought you'd find so many valuable pieces at Romanby Court?'

'Well, I would, obviously,' retorted Cyril, not deceived by her attempt to divert him. 'There might be even prettier pieces out at Watersmeet. I wouldn't know. I've never been inside the place.'

Rachel coloured. 'Watersmeet?' she said faintly, wishing she had seen this coming. 'Oh—you mean the house Ben is thinking of buying,' she appended, realising there was no point in being coy. 'No. I don't think you'd find anything to interest you there, Mr Caldwell. The Armstrongs weren't collectors. At least, I didn't think so.'

Cyril looked disappointed. 'You've been there, then,' he said sourly.

'Didn't you know?' Rachel guessed she had spoiled his attempt to disconcert her. 'Yes. Ben showed me the house a couple of days ago. He wanted my opinion as to whether I thought Daisy would like it.'

And let him make what he likes of that, she thought grimly, glad that her hands were wrapped around her coffee-cup to disguise their shaking. It had taken an immense amount of courage to adopt just such a careless attitude, and she hoped he wouldn't press her and expose her foolish weakness.

The sound of the shop bell came as a welcome relief. Setting down her cup, Rachel brushed through the curtain to attend to their customer. She hoped by the time she came back Cyril might be in a less provoking mood. But the man who was waiting in the sales area did nothing to encourage that expectation.

It was Ben, standing squarely in the middle of the floor, gazing somewhat concentratedly out of the window. Whatever he had come for, he was evidently not looking forward to her appearance, Rachel thought tremulously. But what was he doing here? Did he want her to lose all credibility?

He turned at the sound of the curtains swishing against the arm of a Hepplewhite carver. In dark trousers and a collarless sweatshirt, his hands pushed carelessly into his pockets, he looked relaxed and disturbingly familiar. The image of how he had looked two evenings ago, eyes glazed, mouth sensual, intent on the pursuit of sexual gratification flashed briefly across her mind, and her pulse quickened. Oh, God, had she really sunk so low? A quick tumble in the woods, with no questions asked?

'Hi.'

His dark eyes met hers across a pair of matching armchairs, and she thought how humiliating it was that he should think he could come here and behave as if nothing had happened. Perhaps he'd come to tell her he was leaving. Daisy would be disappointed. She'd been most put out because her father hadn't appeared the night before.

Once again, aware of Cyril's penchant for eavesdropping, Rachel was obliged to be civil. 'Hello.' The word was crisp but she couldn't help it. Her expression alone should have told him he wasn't welcome here.

'Can we talk?'

'Here?' Rachel's response was slightly hysterical, and controlling herself with difficulty she quickly shook her head. 'Are—are you leaving?' she asked, casting a meaningful glance over her shoulder. 'Or—or can I sell you something? We've got some rather nice porcelain in the back.'

Ben's mouth compressed. 'We need to talk,' he said, apparently indifferent to her frantic efforts to make him understand that their conversation could be overheard. 'What time is your lunch break?'

Rachel expelled an unsteady breath. 'I'm afraid I don't know,' she said now, avoiding his compelling gaze. 'Um—I am rather busy——'

'Rachel——'

Her husband's warning use of her name was still echoing round the shop when Mr Caldwell came through the dividing curtain. 'Ben,' he said genially. 'I thought I recognised your voice. How delightful to see you again. Are you still enjoying your holiday?'

'Very much.' But Ben's tone was guarded now, his eyes on Rachel, willing her to look his way.

'Did I hear you inviting Rachel out for lunch?' the old antiques dealer continued now. And then, without waiting for an answer, 'You can have the rest of the morning off, my dear, if you'd like to. As you can see, Ben, we're not busy, and I'd be a very poor fellow if I couldn't do this for a friend.'

Rachel seethed, knowing full well that this was Cyril's way of getting his own back. He must have heard the reluctance in her voice when she spoke to Ben. His smile, and the glinting amusement in his eyes, confirmed it. It would serve him right if she handed in her notice, she thought. She could—if she decided to go to New Zealand.

'I'll get my jacket,' she said tersely, realising there was no point in trying to argue. Even if Ben chose to get the message, Cyril was determined to have his pound of flesh. And perhaps she did need to speak to Ben. He had to understand how humiliated she felt.

'I hear you're thinking of moving back to the district,' Cyril was saying, as she rejoined them, and Ben gave a cursory nod.

'I'm thinking about it,' he agreed, catching Rachel's eye before she could avoid it. 'Has my wife been telling you we went to see a house at Watersmeet on Monday?'

'I didn't have to tell him anything,' she retorted, before she could prevent herself, and then could have bitten out her tongue when Cyril gave a smug smile.

'You know what villages are like, Ben,' he said, giving his assistant a rueful look. 'Your—er—wife is a little touchy this morning. I'm afraid I may be to blame.'

Rachel face was burning when they stepped out into the street, and the look she cast in Ben's direction was eloquent with meaning. 'I suppose you think this is amusing,' she said, lowering her voice when she realised she was attracting attention. 'Have you no more sense than to come to the shop? Do you want Cyril to broadcast the news that we're having lunch together?'

'I don't particularly care what Cyril says,' replied Ben mildly, glancing up and down the High Street. 'And are we having lunch together? After the way you received my invitation, I'd have thought that was in the balance.'

Rachel pressed her lips together. 'You said we needed to talk,' she reminded him, and Ben inclined his head. 'Well——' She squared her shoulders. 'I agree with you. It's time we got some things straight. You can't go on interfering in my life.'

Ben made no response to this, and Rachel wondered if her pronouncement had finally got through to him. Wondered, too, why she didn't feel more relieved if this was so. This was the man who had ruined her life, she reminded herself. She couldn't be feeling sorry for him. Not after what he'd done.

And, in the event, her doubts were unnecessary. Although her bitter words had brought a certain tightness to his mouth, Ben soon recovered himself. 'So,' he said, 'where do you want to eat? Here, at the hotel? Or in Cheltenham? Your mother seemed to enjoy the Heronry. I guess we could go there.'

'Not like this,' said Rachel quickly, aware of the shortcomings of a worn tweed skirt and low-heeled shoes. She had never been to the Heronry, it was true, but it was far too smart an eating place for her to feel comfortable dressed as she was. Besides, it was fifteen miles to Cheltenham. Much too far to go to say her piece.

'All right. Where, then?' enquired Ben evenly, starting along the pavement so that she automatically fell into step beside him. 'Did you rule out the hotel?' His lips twisted. 'We could always eat in the car.'

'Yes.' Rachel bit her lip, weighing the disadvantages of their being completely alone in his car against the obvious advantage of not having to mince her words. Surely, now that he had proved his physical domination over her, she had nothing to fear? Or was she so weak she didn't trust herself?

'Is that an acceptance?'

They had reached the hotel and Rachel could see the Mercedes parked in the yard. Ben obviously didn't intend for them to eat their lunch here. And wherever he took her, they were bound to be alone.

Expelling her breath, she nodded. 'I suppose so.'

'Right.' Ben pulled the car keys out of his pocket. 'I suggest we buy some sandwiches and a couple of cans of beer. Unless you'd prefer Coke. It's all the same to me.'

They eventually bought some sandwiches and four cans of Coke from a garage shop in Lower Morton. Rachel was not so well-known there, and although she told herself she didn't care who knew about their meeting, it was easier not to have to explain what she was doing.

It was nearly twelve by the time they reached their destination. Much to her surprise, Ben had brought them to Crag's Leap, and he got out of the car for a few minutes and walked to the edge of the precipice, looking down into the valley below with a curious air of detachment.

For her part, Rachel stayed where she was, opening the plastic packs of sandwiches, and arranging them on the console between the two front seats. She'd bought cheese and tomato and prawn mayonnaise, but neither choice appealed to her now. She simply wasn't hungry.

Her eyes drifted back to Ben, and she wondered what he was thinking. It was borne in on her suddenly that he might be considering jumping off, and although she told herself she was being stupidly imaginative, she was relieved when he walked back to the car.

At this time of day, there were no other tourists to enjoy the view. It was too early for sightseers, and too light for lovers. Which reassured her, somewhat, though she was not fool enough to think that what had happened at Watersmeet had made them that.

'Cheese or prawn?' she asked, as he came to take his seat beside her. He didn't get into the car exactly. He just sat sideways, with his feet on the grassy sward outside. Which meant he had his back to her, his shoulders hunched over the arms he was resting along his thighs.

'Nothing right now,' he answered, lifting one hand to slide his fingers through his hair. The hand rested at the back of his head for a few moments, plastering the overlong hair to his neck. Then, with a strangely impatient movement, it was withdrawn, and he buried his head in his hands.

Rachel was dismayed. 'What is it?' she asked, her hands moving towards him almost automatically, and then just as quickly withdrawn. 'Are you ill? Don't you feel well? Can I do anything?'

Ben let his breath out on a long sigh, and then straightened. 'Nothing. Everything!' he said obscurely. He glanced at her over his shoulder. 'Don't look so alarmed. I'm not losing my marbles.'

Rachel swallowed. 'I think we should get to the point of this meeting, don't you?'

'Oh, I do.' Ben turned his back on her again, and stared, seemingly unseeingly, into the distance. 'And I think I should start by telling you what I'm doing here.' He paused. 'Rachel, I don't want us to get a divorce.'

Rachel was shocked. 'You're not serious!'

'Why not?' He continued to stare out across the valley. 'We used to be happy together. We can be happy together again. Don't say that you don't want me, because I simply won't believe you.'

'Because of what happened the other night,' Rachel burst out tremulously, and he nodded.

'Partly.'

'Partly!' Rachel nearly choked on the word. 'Ben, just because I let you have sex with me——'

'You didn't *let me* have sex with you,' he broke in harshly, turning to give her a belittling look. 'For God's sake, Rachel, you wanted what happened as much as I did! All right, I instigated it, but it wouldn't have gone as far as it did if you hadn't wanted it, too.'

'That's not true——'

'It is true.' He was angry now. 'For pity's sake, Rachel, be honest with yourself at least. I didn't rape you. I touched you at your invitation. And why did you offer that invitation? Perhaps you should ask yourself that?'

Rachel sniffed. 'I told you why.'

'Oh, yes.' His mouth curled. 'What was that excuse you made?'

'It wasn't an excuse!'

'Something about making out for old times' sake?' He shook his head. 'That was a come-on, if ever I heard it.'

'And you'd know!'

'I've been propositioned in my time,' he conceded evenly.

'I'll bet.'

'That doesn't mean I've followed up on it,' he put in grimly. 'Like—Elena, for example. I never——'

'Oh, please.' Now Rachel pushed open her door and got out of the car, unable to sit still any longer and listen to him twisting the truth for his own ends. She didn't know what his intention was in telling her he didn't want a divorce suddenly, but whatever happened in the future, she refused to be lied to about the past.

It was surprisingly warm out of the car. The seasons seemed to be capricious these days: warm in April, and freezing cold in June. People said it was the hole in the ozone layer, and, short of another alternative, Rachel supposed she must believe them. In any event, at this moment, her body's heat would have melted the ice-caps single handed.

'Rachel...'

She was unaware he had followed her, until she felt the warm draught of his breath against her nape. The plait she invariably wore had slipped over one shoulder, and she thrust it back now, to protect her sensitive skin.

'Rachel...'

He said her name again, stepping past her now, and turning, almost on the rim of the escarpment. In spite of the antipathy she felt towards him, her hands itched to haul him back. If he took an unwary step, he could pitch a hundred feet down into the valley, or else be torn apart by the brambles that grew in such profusion on the slope.

'If—if you've brought me here to talk about Elena, I think you should take me back,' she said, hoping that by taking a backward step herself she would encourage him to come forward. 'I—there's nothing you can say that can change what happened. I don't know what you think you can gain by bringing it up now. We've been separated for two years, Ben. It's a little late to feel conscience-stricken now.'

Ben sighed, but he didn't move away from the edge. 'All right,' he said. 'Let's leave the problem of Elena for now. You tell me: why do you think I came here?'

Rachel thought about saying, to have some lunch, but she didn't feel much like being facetious at the moment. 'To see Daisy,' she said instead, voicing her real opinion. 'And to complicate my life even further. You don't want me, but you don't want anyone else to have me either.'

'You're wrong!' Ben held her gaze with steady eyes. 'I do want you. I've always wanted you. And let's not forget what really happened. You didn't want me.'

Rachel gasped. 'I thought we weren't going to talk about Elena,' she exclaimed bitterly.

'We're not.' With an effort, Ben controlled himself, his gaze dropping briefly to her mouth. And when it did so, she felt as if he'd touched her. She was so intensely aware of him. 'You didn't want me, Rachel. Long before you decided to believe Elena's lies about me. What was it you always used to say? You were afraid I'd give you another baby?'

'With good cause,' cried Rachel raggedly, and Ben sighed.

'I thought we weren't going to talk about Elena,' he reminded her heavily. 'If the girl was pregnant, it was nothing to do with me.'

Rachel shook her head. 'I don't need you to taunt me with how unhappy I was at that time,' she protested. 'You know why I couldn't risk getting pregnant again. You don't know what it's like, losing something that's become a part of you.'

'Don't I?' His expression was pained. 'Forgive me, but wasn't it a part of me, too?'

'It's not the same.' She shivered. 'In any case, I didn't stop loving you. Not then. I just couldn't do it. I couldn't let you——'

'—into your bed.'

'And that was all that mattered, wasn't it?'

'No, dammit, it wasn't,' he swore angrily. 'Rachel, how do you think I felt, being treated like some monster, whose only reason for wanting to be with you was to thrust myself upon you? I couldn't live without you. You thought I couldn't live without sex!'

'Well, that's what it looked like to me,' she retorted, and then coloured when she realised she had indirectly brought Elena into it again, and Ben groaned.

'What do I have to do to prove to you that I wasn't making love to the girl?' he demanded heavily. 'Have you any idea how difficult it is for me—for any man— to prove he's innocent in cases like this? I thought— foolishly, I suppose—that given time you'd at least be prepared to listen to me. But I was wrong, wasn't I? You're just as stubborn as ever. Even after what happened the other night, you still think I betrayed you, don't you?'

CHAPTER TWELVE

RACHEL trembled. She knew she had only to say yes, she still believed that he and Elena had been having an affair, and their marriage would be over. And it was what she wanted, wasn't it? she asked herself. After all she had gone through, why was she hesitating about taking this final step? She couldn't be having doubts now. It was far too late for that. Yet her mouth was dry, and her palms were moist, and her tongue was uneasily silent.

'Well?' he said harshly. 'Do we call it a day?'

Rachel glanced back at the car. 'You haven't had your lunch.'

'I'm not hungry.'

'You ought to eat——'

'Why?' He gave her a scornful look. 'To give you more time to turn the knife?'

'No.' She wrung her hands together. 'If—if you—didn't touch Elena, who did?'

Ben sighed. 'Hasn't it occurred to you yet that Elena might have been pregnant before she came to work for us?'

Rachel stared at him. 'No.'

'I thought not.' He shrugged. 'But she was.'

'How do you——?' Rachel realised after she'd started how stupid that question was and rephrased it. 'How did you find out she was pregnant?'

'She told me. In confidence, of course. And, fool that I was, I believed her when she said she was ashamed and frightened.' He grimaced.

Rachel gasped. 'That can't be true.'

'Why can't it? Because some malicious female decides to break up our marriage and you were prepared to believe her before me? Believe me, Rachel, it took some

153

time for me to forgive you. That you'd condemn me on the evidence of a woman you scarcely knew!'

'Not—not just on that evidence,' said Rachel unsteadily, and Ben scowled.

'You really believed I'd take that little tramp to bed?'

'What else was I supposed to believe? You were in bed, weren't you?'

Ben closed his eyes for a moment. 'Elena was in bed. I'd been taking a shower. She must have heard the water running, and decided it would be a good time to put her plan into operation.'

'What plan?'

'Oh, grow up, Rachel, for God's sake! You know what plan. If you were pregnant, without any obvious means of support, and you thought you could manipulate a situation to your own ends, wouldn't you try it?' His lips twisted. 'No, of course, you wouldn't. But less—shall we say, scrupulous—people would.'

Rachel tensed. 'If that's what you thought, why didn't you say so at the time?'

'I did.' Ben groaned. 'But you wouldn't listen to me. It was far too easy to believe Elena.'

'Then—afterwards——'

'Afterwards, you wouldn't even talk about it.' He paused. 'Look, don't you remember how things were between us at that time? How strained our relationship was? My God, we didn't sleep together. We didn't even share the same room. Some days we didn't even speak. You were in no frame of mind to believe any explanation I might care to make. You'd got it into your head that Elena and I had been having an affair, and you didn't want to hear anything else.'

'So—you're saying you never slept with Elena?'

'I'm not just saying it. It's how it was.' He looked at her pale face and then uttered a savage oath. 'Oh, what's the use? You're so convinced you're right, you simply won't listen to reason.'

Rachel caught her lower lip between her teeth. 'What I don't understand is why you left.'

'Why I left?' Ben snorted. '*I* didn't walk out on our marriage; you did. I waited ten days for you to come back and at least give me a chance to explain, but you didn't. And, as far as I was aware, you had no intention of doing so.'

'So you left.'

'Yes.' He raked an impatient hand through his hair. 'I left.' His lips twisted. 'Then you came back.'

'It wasn't like that.' Rachel was defensive now. 'I'd needed time to think, to decide what I was going to do. I thought you'd still be there at the house. Maybe if you had been, I'd have listened to you then. But you weren't. You'd gone. And as far as I was concerned, you'd taken Elena with you.'

Ben shook his head. 'So we both made mistakes. The difference is, I'm prepared to forgive you for yours.'

Rachel swallowed. 'That's easy for you to say.'

'No. No, it's not,' he denied angrily. 'It's bloody hard, actually, and it's getting harder all the time.'

'It didn't ruin your life?'

'It didn't ruin yours,' he countered. 'I'm not the one who's looking to marry someone else. I'm not the one who's asking for a divorce.'

'You don't have to,' she retorted bitterly, and he frowned.

'What's that supposed to mean?'

'You're a man. What you do isn't scrutinised the same way anything I do is.'

'And what am I supposed to have done? Continued writing? Yes, I've done that. Been successful? That, too, through no fault of my own.'

'What about the affairs you've had since—since you left?'

Ben lips took on a sardonic curve. 'I suppose I should regard that as some progress,' he remarked wryly. 'At least you didn't say since Elena. And, for your information, I've had no long-term relationships since we split up. I've wished I could care about someone else at times, but you're the only woman I've ever wanted.'

Rachel took a backward step. 'How can you say that? I've seen the pictures of you with other women. I've read articles——'

'And when did you start believing everything you read in the papers? After all I've told you. Oh, Rachel, you make me weep.'

'You're telling me you've never been to bed with another woman? In two years! Oh, Ben, I may be naïve but I'm not stupid!'

'Believe what you like. You will anyway.' He sounded inestimably weary. 'But don't tell me you love this guy Barrass, because I won't believe you. When we made love the other evening, I knew it was as much a new experience for you as it was for me. I never intended it to happen. I took you there, to the house, to tell you what I'm telling you now. Only things got—out of hand. I'm not sorry it happened.' He rocked back on his heels and Rachel's nerves, already shredded by the doubts he had invoked, were stretched to screaming pitch. 'Hell, it proved to me you were still the Rachel I used to know, the Rachel I married. But—I guess you thought I'd taken advantage of you, and that's why I didn't force the issue when I came round last night.'

Rachel blinked, briefly diverted from the terrifying image she had of Ben falling. 'You came round last night? But my mother——'

'I came to the house,' he amended softly. 'But I didn't come in. There was a Range Rover parked in the drive, and I guessed it belonged to Barrass. Then I saw the two of you come out and get into it, and I made myself scarce. In any case, I was so sick that you obviously intended going on with your relationship with him, I knew I was in no condition to state my case convincingly.' He paused. 'That's why I came to the shop this morning. Not to upset you or embarrass you, but because I couldn't take the risk that you might be seeing him again tonight.'

Rachel bent her head. 'I'm not.'

'No?' He shrugged. 'Well, I wasn't to know that.'

'No.'

Rachel lifted her head, and as she did so, another car turned into the parking area. It was apparently some tourists, come to take a look at the view, and although she knew she should feel grateful, Rachel wished they'd chosen any place but here.

Ben swore then audibly and succinctly. Obviously, they couldn't continue their conversation now, and he kicked savagely at a tussock of grass, causing the ground beneath his feet to crumble dangerously.

Afterwards, Rachel chided herself that he had been in no real danger. Even if he had lost his footing, there would surely have been time to lunge for safety. But prior events had left her in a state of some agitation, and when she saw his feet slipping, she leapt forward and hauled him back.

It happened so quickly, she didn't really think either of them could have planned it. All she knew was, that when she grasped his hand, she felt an instinctive need to hold on. And Ben seemed to respond to her uncertainty. With a muffled groan, he dragged her into his arms.

With one hand at her throat and the other behind her head, he brought her mouth roughly to his, kissing her as if he'd never let her go. Hard, and passionate, his lips took and possessed hers with uncontrolled hunger, letting her feel the frustration he'd been suppressing for so long.

Rachel felt herself leaning into him, felt her limbs yielding and moulding themselves to the hard contours of his body. Time, place, even her reason, swam away from her. He kissed her as if there had been no past, would be no future, unless they were together.

And then, as if the sound of a car door slamming, and the muted murmur of voices was one intrusion too

many, he let her go. As Rachel struggled to come to terms
with his withdrawal, Ben strode silently back to the car.
By the time she had gathered what little composure she
had left, dipped her head in embarrassed acknowledg-
ment of the elderly couple, who had left their car to
marvel at the depth of the escarpment, he had started
the engine, and as soon as she'd scrambled inside, he
drove away. The tyres spun on the stony surface of the
parking area, as he performed a violent three-point turn,
and then he swung out on to the country road that led
back to Upper Morton and sanity.

The sandwiches and the cans of Coke had been tossed
carelessly into the back of the car, but Rachel couldn't
honestly say she was sorry. The smell of the food in the
warm car was fairly nauseating to her outraged senses,
and coming on top of what had happened, it caused a
quivery feeling in her stomach.

'I'll be leaving in the morning,' he said, as she was
desperately trying to think of something to say, and her
lips parted.

'Leaving?'

'Yes. That's what you want, isn't it? I'll instruct my
solicitor to give yours whatever assistance is necessary,
and as soon as the papers are filed, I'll have Ferrars send
the deeds of Wychwood to you.'

'What?' Rachel was staggered.

'Wychwood,' said Ben tightly, concentrating on the
road. 'The house is yours. I had it put in your name just
after the separation.' His lips twisted. 'I wanted you to
have some sort of security. Just in case anything happened to me. Probate can take some time.'

Rachel shook her head. 'But it's your house.'

'It's not. It's yours. You can sell it, if you like. I don't
care. Tell Barrass it's my wedding present to you. I
daresay it won't be much use to you after you're married
and you and Daisy are living at Kingsmead.'

CHAPTER THIRTEEN

RACHEL'S mother came to find her after supper that evening.

Rachel hadn't said much during the meal, but luckily Daisy had been full of excitement about the coming jumble sale at the school.

'I gave Miss Gregory your note,' she said, 'and she was really pleased you'd offered to help out. Do you think Daddy might come, too? As he's staying in the village, you wouldn't mind, would you?'

'He's not staying in the village,' Rachel answered quickly, meeting her mother's eyes half defensively. 'I—I spoke to him at lunchtime, and he says he's going back to town tomorrow.'

Of course, Daisy had been disappointed, and it had been left to Mrs Collins to comfort the little girl. But Rachel had been too much in need of comfort herself to console her daughter, and it had been that look of anguish in her face that had brought her mother to her bedroom.

'What are you doing?' Mrs Collins asked, pausing in the doorway, and Rachel looked up half guiltily from the album of family photos in her lap.

'Nothing much,' she said, closing the book on the wealth of snapshots from their honeymoon. Ben had practically bankrupted himself taking her to Tahiti, but she'd never forget those velvet-soft nights in the Polynesian paradise.

'Nothing?' her mother echoed, stepping casually into the room. 'Since when have you spent your evenings weeping over old photographs?'

Rachel scrubbed the heels of her hands across her eyes. 'I'm not weeping.'

'All right.' Her mother didn't argue. She perched on the opposite side of the bed from where Rachel was sitting, cross-legged, and eyed the heavy album across her knees. 'Anything interesting?'

'Not really.' Rachel put the book aside. 'Where's Daisy?'

'Watching television.' Mrs Collins hesitated. 'Um—what did Ben say at lunchtime? You weren't very forthcoming about why he wanted to see you.'

Rachel sniffed, wishing she wasn't so transparent. 'He—he just wanted to tell me he's turned this house over to me. We can go on living here as long as we like.'

'You mean—until the divorce?'

'Yes.' Rachel smoothed her fingers over her jean-clad knees. 'He's agreed to that, too.'

'Ben has?'

'Who else?' She avoided her mother's gaze.

'But—the last time I spoke to Ben, I got the impression that was the last thing he wanted.'

'Yes.' Rachel sighed. 'Well, he's changed his mind.'

'Why?'

'Oh, Mum!'

'You might as well tell me. I'm going to sit here until I find out. Have he and—Simon—had a bust-up or something? I knew that man was trouble as soon as I laid eyes on him.'

'Ben?'

'Don't be obtuse, Rachel. You know perfectly well who I'm talking about. Simon. Simon Barrass. Not content with upsetting you, he's obviously made trouble with Ben as well.'

'No, he hasn't.' Rachel propped her elbows on her knees, and pushed both hands into her hair. Then, because she knew there was no way she was going to convince her mother of what she was saying without telling the truth, she said wearily, 'Simon and I are finished. We broke up last night, if you must know. My seeing Ben had nothing to do with Simon. He—I—oh, he insisted on rehashing all that old stuff about Elena. He says she was pregnant before she came to work for us. He says she came to our room deliberately. I guess, if his story is true, she hoped she could get him to make love to her, and pass the baby off as his.'

Mrs Collins bent her head. 'I see.'

'Did he tell you that?'

'Ben hasn't talked about what happened to me,' replied her mother evenly. 'Though I have to say, if he had, I'd have been inclined to listen. He seemed genuinely cut up about you wanting a divorce. If he was half as bad as you believe, I'd have thought he'd have jumped at the chance to gain his freedom.'

'Yes.' Rachel said the word unhappily. 'I'd have thought that, too.'

'What about Elena? What happened to her?'

'He says he doesn't know. He says he hasn't seen her since that morning I walked out.'

'Mmm.' Mrs Collins was thoughtful. 'You only have his word for that, of course.'

'I only have his word for everything. That's the trouble,' said Rachel vehemently. 'Oh, what am I going to do? If he goes back to London, I'll never see him again.'

'And that matters?' Her mother was tentative.

Rachel hesitated, and then she nodded. 'Yes. Yes, damn him, it matters.' She lifted her head and gazed at her mother with tear-bright eyes. 'What would you say if I told you I was thinking of taking him back? I can't help it. I still love him. I don't think I've ever stopped.'

'I'd say, then why are you sitting here, moping over his old photographs, when you could be telling him what you've just told me? Oh, my dear, marriage is about trust, as well as commitment. And Ben has proved he loves you, by giving you your freedom.'

'Now are you sure you're going to be all right?' Mrs Collins hesitated beside the taxi that had come to take her to Cheltenham station to catch her train. 'I don't like leaving you alone at present, but I've really got to start sorting out my own affairs.'

'And I'm not alone,' Rachel pointed out firmly, squashing the panicky feeling she felt at the realisation that her life had gone so drastically wrong. 'I've got Daisy. And Mr Caldwell. And one or two good friends I can rely on. Besides, we'll be coming up to London ourselves in a week or so. When Daisy has her mid-term break, I promise we'll spend the holiday with you.'

'Be sure you do.' There were tears in Mrs Collins' eyes as she kissed her daughter goodbye. 'And promise me you won't do anything silly, like allowing that ignorant farmer back into your life. And do think seriously about accepting our invitation. You heard what Ralph said on the phone last night.'

'I know.' Rachel smiled. 'And I will think about it. Now, come on, you've got to get going. Do you want to miss your train?'

She waved until the taxi had disappeared along Stoneberry Lane, and then turned and went back into the house. In spite of what she had said, it was horribly empty suddenly, and she wished now that she'd allowed Daisy to take the day off school as she'd wanted. But, since Ben's departure, their relationship had been decidedly shaky, and she knew her daughter blamed her for Ben's leaving as he did.

The fact that Rachel had been as shocked by his sudden departure as anyone meant nothing. In Daisy's eyes, Rachel was to blame, and nothing her mother could say would convince her that it wasn't so.

Yet Rachel had suffered terribly when she discovered Ben had left the afternoon after their visit to Crag's Leap. Although she had confessed how she felt about Ben to her mother, it had taken an enormous amount of courage to go to the hotel to tell him so. And then, when she'd got there, she'd found that he'd already left the Old Swan. As far as Charlie Braddock knew, his famous guest

had returned to London. 'Didn't even leave a for-
warding address,' he grumbled. 'Though I guess you'd
know where he lives, wouldn't you, Mrs Leeming?'

And, of course, she did. But she also knew she didn't
have the courage to go and seek Ben out in London.
She'd never been to the house he owned in Elton Square,
and it was far too late to think she ever could.

Of course, her mother had tried to persuade her. She
had even stayed on over the weekend, so that she could
attend the jumble sale at Daisy's school in Rachel's place,
should her daughter decide to go to London. But, in
spite of her mother's pleas, and Daisy's belligerence, she
hadn't left the village. Except to help out at the jumble
sale on Saturday, she conceded. When she'd been half
afraid that Ben would join them, and half afraid he
wouldn't.

He hadn't. She hadn't really expected he would. So
far as Ben was concerned, this particular episode of his
life was at last over. All she was waiting for now was
the letter from his solicitors, informing her that he was
sueing for a divorce. She had the feeling he'd do it that
way. Rather than wait for her to make the first move.

She glanced at her watch. It was nearly one o'clock.
Cyril had given her an extended lunch hour so that she
could see her mother off, and she wasn't due back for
another hour at least. Time enough to run a Hoover
over the spare bedroom carpet. And to strip off the
sheets, and put them in the washer, she thought firmly.

It didn't take long. Her mother was not an untidy
person, and in no time at all Rachel had removed the
sheets and hoovered the carpet. Perhaps she should do
Daisy's bedroom carpet and her own as well, she reflected, well aware that she was keeping busy to avoid
thinking of other things. But she'd got over Ben before,
she told herself severely. She'd get over him again.

It was as she was vacuuming her own bedroom carpet
that she found the photograph. It must have fallen from
between the pages of the album, when she was looking

at it the other evening. She couldn't believe it had ever occupied a permanent place in the album, but she remembered Elena sending it to them at the time she applied for the job.

It was hard to look at the girl who had caused such a disastrous upheaval in her life, but Rachel forced herself to do it, telling herself, quite objectively, that Elena was no longer to blame for their estrangement. She was. It was her fault that Ben had gone away, her fault that he had lost the will to care. She had had her chance; two chances, actually, and she had blown them both. Her love had been so brittle, it had shattered at the first sign of a flaw.

Blinking, she held the picture up to the light. It showed a girl standing in front of a house, with the sun slanting down on to a stone basin at her side. The snapshot had been taken with a wide-angle lens, and it was possible to see quite a lot of the house, too. Strangely, the building looked familiar, and it wasn't until she'd studied it more closely that she realised she'd seen it before.

It was the house at Watersmeet, the house Ben had taken her to see last week. My God! The name he had used when he told her who owned the house suddenly came back to her. And it had been some people called Armstrong who had given Elena a reference.

She trembled, as something else Ben had said flickered in her memory. He'd mentioned that one of the Armstrongs' sons was divorced, because of some trouble with an au pair. She'd thought he'd been joking at the time, and she'd never taken him up on it. But now she couldn't help the suspicion that he'd had some other reason for taking her to see the house.

What was it he'd said? That he'd taken her there to tell her what he'd eventually told her that day at Crag's Leap? But that things had got out of hand and—well, she knew very well what had happened then. He must have hoped she would make the connection. He must have hoped she would realise what he had done. But, oh, God, she had been so wrapped up in him and what he was doing, she hadn't even remembered the family's name.

But she remembered it now. Remembered the glowing reference they had given their erstwhile helper. They must have been heartily glad to see the back of her, thought Rachel bitterly. If she'd known what was going to happen, she'd have written her a glowing reference herself.

With a feeling of despair, she tore the picture into shreds now, and going into the adjoining bathroom, she flushed it down the toilet. So much for Elena Dupois, she thought painfully. If only she'd believed Ben instead of her.

There was a phone message from her mother, when she got back from work that evening, saying she had arrived home safely, and that she had had a good journey. 'I wish I could go and stay with Nana,' said Daisy sulkily, pushing the peas and carrots round her plate. 'Then she might take me to see Daddy. It's awful living here when he's in London.'

Rachel suppressed her own feelings, and forced a tight smile. 'It's never bothered you before.'

'Yes, it has. Only then I used to think that if you and Daddy could get together again, you'd realise it had all been a mistake. The—the separation, I mean. Hazel Kendrick says you probably split up over another woman. Her father and mother are divorced, because Mr Kendrick was found in bed with his secretary.'

Rachel was appalled. 'Hazel had no business discussing such things with you,' she exclaimed, but Daisy was unrepentant.

'Why not? It's what happens, isn't it? Hazel says it's going on all the time.' She shrugged. 'But I said it was you and not Daddy who'd found someone else.'

'Daisy!' Rachel was horrified, as much by the revelation of her daughter's worldliness, as by any sense of indignation on her own behalf. 'Anyway, if you must

know, my relationship with Simon—with Mr Barrass—
is over. We won't be selling this house, and we won't be
moving to Kingsmead.'

'Do you mean it?'

Daisy was clearly delighted, and Rachel supposed it
relieved a little of her own misery to see her daughter
looking cheerful once again. It was a small price to pay
to keep her happy.

And during the next couple of days, Rachel did her
best to maintain a cheerful disposition. Even though
Cyril's digs about Ben soon getting bored in Upper
Morton began to get on her nerves. It was as if her being
proved right over the Russian icon was a constant irritation, and he did everything he could to make her feel
small.

Then, on Thursday, she had a bad fall.

As usual, the room at the back of the shop was
crammed with boxes and bric-a-brac, and Rachel had
been balancing on a rickety pair of steps when they gave
way. With a startled cry, she fell among an assortment
of Chinese vases and picture frames, twisting her back
quite badly, and cutting her arm on one of the vases.

The noise of pictures falling, and the steps crashing
down among a pile of model cars, brought Mr O'Shea
rushing in from the warehouse. Cyril, who had been at-
tending to a customer at the time, came through just as
Rachel was getting to her feet, and predictably, his first
concern was for his stock.

'Whatever were you doing?' he exclaimed, hurrying
forward to rescue the remains of the porcelain vase.
'Good heavens, do you know how much this was worth?'

'As it's Qianlong, I'd say about half a K,' replied Mr
O'Shea shortly, before Rachel could offer any apology.
'The girl's hurt, Cyril. Shouldn't you be worried in case
she asks for compensation?'

'Oh, really——' began Rachel, flexing her back
muscles with tentative care, but Cyril's attention had
been caught by the old restorer.

'Half a K,' he echoed. 'Oh, I don't understand all this modern jargon.' He examined the broken vase ruefully. 'It could have been Kangxi.'

'But it's not,' said Mr O'Shea impatiently. 'Here: take Rachel's other arm. We'll help her on to the sofa.'

'But that's a George III sofa,' protested Cyril, before Mr O'Shea's expression had him hurrying to obey. 'Oh, dear, Rachel, you haven't really hurt yourself, have you? I've warned you about overreaching yourself. You should have moved the canvases out of the way to make it easier.'

Rachel forbore from mentioning that she would have had to move the picture frames, the canvases, and all the other bits and pieces lying about the floor, before she could have put her steps near enough to reach the shelves she was clearing without a struggle. And, as the floor was already overflowing with stock anyway, it would have been virtually impossible to find an empty space.

'Never mind about that now.' Mr O'Shea had taken charge of the situation, and he sent Cyril off to make Rachel a cup of strong sweet tea, while he dealt with the cut on her arm. Happily, it wasn't deep, and after bathing it in clean water, some antiseptic cream and a bandage sufficed. But she did feel rather shaken, and she wasn't sorry when Mr O'Shea suggested to Cyril that she should be allowed to take the rest of the day off.

'I wouldn't come back until Monday, if I were you,' he averred, ignoring Cyril's thoroughly outraged impotence. 'That was quite a fall, and it might be wise to rest your back for a couple of days. I'm sure Mr Caldwell would rather you did that than have you sueing him later for a slipped disc.'

And, of course, Cyril had to agree, although he prefaced his endorsement by insisting that she'd only herself to blame. But the fact remained that the working conditions in the shop were distinctly hazardous, and with Mr O'Shea's encouragement he promised to get one of the larger auction houses to come and clear some of the less valuable items.

In consequence, Rachel was home by lunchtime, with strict instructions not to do anything energetic for the next seventy-two hours. 'You have to think of Daisy,' said Cyril, with one of his typically false displays of concern. 'Who would look after her, if you had to go into hospital?' he added, when what he was really saying was that she couldn't afford to lose her job.

Thinking of her daughter reminded Rachel that she ought to ring Lady's Mount, and ask them to tell Daisy to come straight home after school. The head teacher, Mrs Latimer, was most concerned when she heard why Rachel was making the call, and she offered her best wishes, and the hope that she'd soon be feeling better.

That done, Rachel made herself a cup of coffee, hesitating only a moment before adding a second spoonful of sugar. What price worrying about her weight now? she thought, as she changed from her skirt and blouse into casual clothes. There was no one to care if she was fat or thin, or reproach her if she ate too many sweet things.

Her image, in a pair of baggy sweatpants and an old shirt of Ben's she'd rescued from the bottom of his closet after he'd moved out, was not inspiring. She'd originally intended to tear the shirt up and use it for cleaning jobs, but it was so soft and comfortable to wear that she'd relented. Nevertheless, she was glad she wasn't expecting any company. Apart from her appearance, her back was feeling rather stiff.

She was lying on the sofa in the snug, wondering if she had time to take a bath before Daisy got home, when her doorbell rang. A glance at her watch assured her that it couldn't be her daughter. Not yet. And anyone else was just unwelcome.

Hoping whoever it was wouldn't decide to look through the window, she pretended she hadn't heard anything. It was probably just someone selling brushes. If she didn't show her face they'd go away.

The bell rang again, this time accompanied by the rattle of the letter-box. 'Rachel!' Oh, God, it was Simon's voice. 'Rachel, I know you're in there. Come on, Rachel,' he was more wheedling now. 'I've brought you something to make you feel better.'

It would have been all the same if she'd been in bed, thought Rachel wearily, rolling rather painfully off the couch. And whatever he'd brought, it was unlikely to make her feel better. She'd hoped she'd seen the last of him. She really thought he'd have got the message by now.

She looked at her watch again. She must have been asleep, because it was almost half-past three. Daisy would be home in half an hour. If only Simon could have held off until then.

When she opened the door, it was only wide enough for him to see her face. She had no intention of inviting him in. No intention of accepting anything except his apologies for disturbing her. Even the bunch of flowers in his hand, which he thrust towards her as soon as she was visible, were an unwarranted intrusion into her privacy. What was he doing here anyway? How had he known where to find her?

The answer was obvious, of course, and she didn't need his rapid explanation to understand it. 'Cyril said you needed cheering up,' he added, his fair face flushed and defensive. 'I saw him at lunchtime, in the Swan. I thought it was a good time to make amends.'

Rachel leaned heavily on the door, making no attempt to take the flowers, and his hand fell awkwardly to his side again. 'No amends are necessary,' she said evenly. 'I think we both made a mistake. Me, for thinking I loved you, and you, for proving I didn't.'

Simon's face darkened. 'Am I supposed to understand that?'

Rachel expelled her breath on a sigh. 'It's the truth. I'm afraid I let the prospect of financial security blind me to the real extent of my feelings. I liked you, Simon. I even think I was fond of you. But, you must agree, we did have different agendas.'

'I don't agree.' Simon's jaw jutted. He glanced over her shoulder. 'Aren't you going to invite me in?'

'I don't think so.' Rachel hoped he wouldn't make an issue of it. 'We don't have anything to say to one another. It was—fun, but it's over. I'm sorry. I hope we can remain friends.'

Simon scowled. 'It's Leeming, isn't it?' he exclaimed, taking an aggressive step forward. 'Ever since he came back, you've been acting like a fool. Good God, the man cuckolded you! He was having it off with that French nursemaid, who everyone knew was bound to cause trouble. Heavens, she'd already caused ructions between Harry Armstrong and his wife. So much so that his mother had threatened to have her deported!'

Rachel felt sick. 'How do you know this?'

'It was common knowledge at the lodge.' Simon was very proud of the fact that he was a Freemason, and it wasn't the first time he had spoken of the camaraderie that existed within the order. 'The Armstrongs always did consider themselves better than the rest of us. Harry's father—old man Armstrong, that is—used to act like he owned half the county.'

Rachel moistened her lips. 'And you resented that.'

'Well, wouldn't you? We were all glad when they left the district.'

'Which was when?'

'Does it matter?'

'I'd like to know.'

Simon sighed. 'Oh, well—not that long ago, actually. Soon after that trouble between you and your husband, I think it was. I know the house has been on the market for some time. I also heard that, in spite of all his mother's efforts, Harry had to marry the girl eventually.

There was talk that she was pregnant, and that they went to live in France, with her family.'

Rachel stared at him. 'Why didn't you tell me this before?'

'I didn't think it would interest you.' Simon shrugged. 'The subject did seem kind of sensitive to broach. I'm only telling you now to prove what a bastard your husband was. For heaven's sake, Rachel, going to bed with a pregnant woman! If that doesn't show what a swine he is, I'd like to know what does.'

CHAPTER FOURTEEN

SHE got rid of him somehow. It wasn't easy, and Rachel
was sure Simon still believed she'd change her mind
about him, after she'd had time to think. It was a
measure of his conceit that he didn't regard the way he
had treated her as in any way comparable to the way
Ben was supposed to have acted. That they had both
deceived her was evident. That Ben's deceit was a result
of her own intolerance was almost impossible to bear.

She made herself another cup of coffee, knowing the
caffeine wasn't doing her nervous system any good, but
desperate for something to fill the emptiness inside her.
She wasn't hungry. For all her fears of getting fat, she
hadn't eaten a proper meal since her mother left. And
even before that she had only picked at her food. What
she needed was sustenance, but not the edible kind.

It was nearly half-past four before she realised that
Daisy should have been home by now. School finished
at half-past three, and after allowing time for the children
to collect their coats and their belongings, the mini-bus
usually left at about twenty minutes to four. Then, with
no hold-ups, and not forgetting the couple of stops he
made along the way, the driver usually managed to drop
Daisy home at about five minutes past four. Occasionally
it had been ten past, but never as late as this.

Rachel's throat felt dry. Oh, God, she had been so
wrapped up in her own misery, she'd actually forgotten
all about her daughter. Surely Mrs Latimer had given
her the message? She couldn't be at the shop, could she?
Cyril would have phoned.

Even so, knowing she had to check all possibilities
before getting into a panic, Rachel forced herself to go
into the hall and pick up the phone. Let it just be a

mistake, she prayed urgently. Please, oh, please, don't let anything bad have happened to her.

Her own aches and pains forgotten for the moment, she was dialling Cyril's number when she heard the sound of a car turn into the drive. It wasn't familiar, and briefly the thought that it might be the police, come to report an accident, kept her frozen to the spot.

But then common sense asserted itself, and putting down the receiver again, she went stiffly to the door. It could be Cyril, she told herself. She had to stop thinking the worst.

The sight of Ben, getting out of the grey Mercedes, almost caused her heart to stop beating altogether. Daisy wasn't with him. She saw that straight away. And she could think of no reason for Ben to be here, unless he was the bearer of bad news.

Clinging desperately to the doorframe, she said her daughter's name, hardly aware of the tears on her cheeks, until Ben leapt up the steps towards her. 'She's OK,' he said huskily. 'She's with my secretary.' He brushed a tear from her cheek with a gentle hand. 'I'm sorry if you were worried. I'm afraid there was a hold-up on the M40.'

Rachel blinked, half afraid that if she let go of the frame her legs would give out on her. 'A hold-up?' she echoed faintly. 'But I—I don't understand.'

'You will,' said Ben gently, gesturing into the hall behind her. 'Shall we go inside? I don't feel inclined to give Mrs Reynolds anything else to gossip about, do you?'

Rachel shook her head, and moved obediently aside, so that he could come in. It occurred to her, as the ache in her back reasserted itself, that she hadn't even hesitated before letting him in. Was she really that desperate to see him? She was rather afraid she was.

'Are you all right?'

He'd halted in the hall, tall and disturbingly attractive in those familiar surroundings. And his first words, once

the door was closed, brought the foolish tears to her
eyes again. The fact that he had asked the question
proved that someone must have told him about her fall.
It could only have been Daisy, and Rachel hoped he
didn't think she had had anything to do with it.

So, 'I'm fine,' she managed briskly, making a determined effort to walk normally along the hall. Her back
protested at the sudden exertion as she turned into the
living-room. 'I—I'm sorry Daisy troubled you. As you
can see, I'm on the mend.'

'Are you?' Ben followed her into the room, and she
was aware of his eyes watching her like a hawk. The
knowledge made her clumsy, and without waiting for
him to join her she sank down weakly on to the sofa.
'Daisy didn't—trouble me,' he added. 'Your mother
phoned me, actually. She thought I ought to know.'

Rachel blinked. 'My mother? But, how——?'

'All right.' Ben came to stand behind the sofa, and
Rachel shuffled to the edge of the seat almost instinctively. 'Daisy did contact her grandmother. She was
worried about you, and I think Mrs Latimer thought it
was a good idea.' He rested his hands on the smooth
fabric, and moulded it, unthinkingly. 'I told Daisy to
wait for me at the school, and I got down here as soon
as I could.'

'There was no need...'

Rachel lifted her shoulders helplessly, wondering why
it was that Ben always saw her at her worst. Oh, he
looked a little dishevelled himself, with his hair rumpled
by the wind—or by the raking movement of his hands,
she couldn't be sure—and the shadow of his beard darkening his jawline, but he still looked sexy, and too desirable to be true.

'Wasn't there?' he asked now, and to her alarm he
came round the sofa and seated himself beside her. The
cushion, depressed by his weight, tilted alarmingly, and
she clutched the arm of the sofa tightly, to prevent herself
from falling into his arms. 'What happened?'

His tone was so gentle that Rachel had to look down at her knees to prevent him from seeing the stupid weakness in her eyes. Oh, God, she just wasn't up to dealing with him now.

'I—nothing much,' she mumbled, in answer, touching her hair with a nervous hand, and then stopping herself from doing so. 'I—had a fall, that's all. I got a shock more than anything else. The only reason I rang the school was to let Daisy know where I was.'

'How did you fall?'

'From some steps.' Rachel made a distracted gesture. 'Where is Daisy anyway? You said——'

'I said she was with my secretary, and she is. Karen's very good with children. It probably comes from the fact that she's had three of her own, plus a couple of grandchildren.'

'Grandchildren?'

Rachel was surprised, and Ben pulled a wry face. 'I know,' he said. 'You thought she was blonde and beautiful, didn't you?' He grinned. 'Well, she is, I suppose. Blonde, anyway. But forty-six if she's a day, and very happily married.'

Rachel coloured. 'I never...' Her voice trailed away. He'd known she was lying. 'So—where are they?' She frowned. 'Not waiting in the car!'

'Can you see that?' Ben's tone was dry. 'Our daughter sitting meekly in the car while we talked? No. I dropped the pair of them off in Cheltenham. Karen's taking her shopping, and then they're going to get some tea. I wanted to speak to you without interruption. And we both know how impossible that is, if Daisy's around.'

Rachel quivered. 'But—how will they get back?'

Ben's mouth compressed. 'Let Karen worry about that, will you? They'll get a taxi, I guess. You'll find she's quite efficient when you get to know her.'

Rachel bent her head again. 'I'm sure she is,' she said, letting go of the arm of the sofa to smooth her damp palms over her knees. 'And—it was—kind of you to be so—so concerned——'

Ben swore then, so that she broke off what she was saying to stare at him with half fearful eyes. 'It wasn't *kind* at all,' he said harshly, spreading his legs and running agitated hands up and down his thighs. 'For God's sake, Rachel——' his eyes searched her face, dark and frustrated '—I was worried about you, dammit! When your mother said you and Barrass had broken up, I felt bloody responsible!'

Rachel's lips parted. 'My mother had no right——'

'Yes, she did. She had every right.' Ben was breathing unevenly now. 'She knew how I felt about you. Knew that anything concerning you would concern me.' He paused. 'What happened? Did he find out about us going to Watersmeet, or did that employer of yours happen to tell him that I'd come to the shop looking for you the other day? It's the sort of thing Cyril would do, the old bastard! Well, if you're expecting me to say I'm sorry, I shouldn't hold your breath!'

Rachel trembled. 'Simon knows—nothing about us. He—he suspects. But—it's nothing to do with him any longer.'

Ben stared at her. 'So—do you want me to talk to him?' he asked tersely, and Rachel almost choked.

'What?'

'I said do you want me to talk to him?' Ben was very tense, his hands lying along his thighs now, still, but not relaxed, as Rachel could see. 'I will if you want me to. I'll tell him how it was. That it was all my fault. If the fool has any sense, he'll forgive you.'

Rachel expelled her breath on a shivery sigh. 'And— and what if I don't want him to forgive me?' she asked unsteadily, as the realisation that she was being given another chance, too, began to dawn on her dazed senses, and Ben frowned.

'Am I supposed to understand that?' he asked stiffly. 'Rachel, your mother said——'

'Yes?' Suddenly, she felt a wave of confidence sweeping over her. 'What did my mother say? Did she tell you I went to see you? Did she tell you I went to the hotel?'

Ben blinked. 'No.' He shook his head. 'What hotel?'

Rachel straightened her spine, feeling the little twinge it gave, but not really caring suddenly. 'The Old Swan, of course,' she replied softly. 'But—you'd gone back to London.'

Ben stared at her with guarded eyes. 'You went to the Swan?' he echoed. 'When?'

Rachel swallowed a little nervously. 'That evening. The evening after—after we'd—talked.'

'Why?'

Rachel moved her shoulders. 'Why did you leave?' she asked, instead of answering him, and Ben's fingers dug grimly into his thighs.

'You know why,' he said harshly. 'There's only so much a man can take without losing his self-respect, as well as his reason. When I left here, I never wanted to see you again. You and I were finished. This time, I thought, for good!'

Rachel wet her dry lips with a tentative tongue. 'So—so why did you come back?'

'God, you know that too!' he grated roughly. 'Your mother only had to hint that you might be injured, or in pain, and I couldn't wait to drop everything and get down here.' He lifted one hand and ran frustrated fingers through his hair. 'That's what you do to me, damn you. What you've always done to me. That's why I found it so inconceivable that you could—oh, damn! What's the use?'

Rachel hesitated only a moment, and then she laid her hand on his knee. The muscle jumped beneath her fingers, and she felt the stiffness that invaded his bones at her touch. But instead of responding to his withdrawal, she finger-walked along his thigh, until his hand came down, imprisoning hers against his leg.

'Don't.'

'Why not?' She looked into his eyes. 'Don't you like it?'

His mouth twisted. 'Is this a game, Rachel? Have you suddenly devised some new way to make me squirm? Look...' He held up his free hand. 'If you've got something to say, say it. Don't make a fool of me. I can do that too easily for myself.'

'Oh, Ben...' Rachel gazed at him achingly. 'Can't you guess why I went to the hotel? Can't you see what I'm trying to convey?'

'Was this before or after Barrass threw you out?' he demanded savagely, and with a little cry of horror Rachel snatched her hand from his grasp.

'You'd better leave,' she choked, getting up from the couch and stumbling across the room. 'Go on. Get out! I never want to see you again!'

He caught her before she reached the door, his hands hard and unyielding on her upper arms as he hauled her back against him. 'I'm sorry, I'm sorry,' he muttered burying his face in the hollow between her neck and her shoulder, pressing her so close to him she could feel he was trembling, too. 'It's only because I love you so much,' he added brokenly. 'And I've been hurt so often, I couldn't help hurting you, too.'

Rachel stood there, feeling his lips against her neck, feeling the warmth of his hands gripping her arms, and the heat of his body at her back, and knew she couldn't fight her feelings any longer. This was her husband, her destiny; the only man she had ever loved.

And so she let herself lean into him, let the sensual warmth of his nearness surround her. His body was so lean and hard, so familiar. She wanted to be closer to him. She wanted to satisfy the needs he could so effortlessly inspire.

His hands slid round her waist, brushing her flat stomach before finding the hem of the old shirt, and sliding up to her bare midriff. His thumbs stroked the undersides of her breasts, causing her nipples to strain helplessly against the cloth. Then, as if sensing her urgency, he took her breasts in his hands, squeezing them gently, before massaging the aching peaks against his palms.

She let out a sound then, a cry, that caught in her throat, and betrayed its vulnerability. Waves of heat, of fire, of need, were sweeping over her. She was drowning in their hunger, she was aching with their sweetness.

'Si—Simon didn't—throw me out,' she got out tremulously as Ben's tongue made a sensuous exploration of her ear, and she felt him give a sigh.

'It doesn't matter,' he said unsteadily. 'I don't care why you tried to see me, so long as you did.' He turned her in his arms, looking down possessively as his fingers made short work of her shirt buttons. 'Oh, Rachel—whatever you do, don't send me away again. I don't think I could stand it.'

'Nor could I,' she admitted, her hands cupping his face, stroking his cheek, feeling the slight roughness of his beard against her palms. 'But let me tell you what happened. I want you to know why I went to the hotel.'

'All right.'

With an obvious effort Ben contained his impatience, fastening at least two of her buttons again before taking her hand and drawing her back to the sofa. This time, he sat down first and pulled her on to his lap. But she could feel the swollen hardness of him, pressing against her bottom, and it was incredibly difficult to concentrate on other things when she so badly wanted him there, inside her.

'Go on,' he said, nuzzling her neck, and although she lifted her shoulder to facilitate his efforts she forced herself to speak.

'I—I'd broken up with Simon before we went to Crag's Leap that morning,' she confessed, thereby focusing his attention. 'We had a row, the night after—after you'd

taken me to Watersmeet. I—wouldn't let him touch me.
As you'd guessed, he never had.'

'Why?'

Ben's tone was almost matter-of-fact, but a glance at
his face warned her he was not as indifferent as he
seemed. His eyes were dark and glittering, and there was
a tenseness about his expression that was as forbidding
as it was exciting.

'Because I didn't love him,' she answered softly. 'Because, after you made love to me, I knew I could never
do that with anyone else. I might want to hate you, and
believe me, there have been times when I've come close,
but I never did. I know it's taken far too long, but I
wanted you back in my life.'

Ben's exhalation was slow and cautious. 'Wanted?' he
echoed warily, and she hurried to reassure him.

'Want,' she amended urgently. 'I want you back in
my life. If—if you'll forgive me. For all the pain I've
put us through.'

Ben smoothed a strand of her hair between his fingers.
'What made you change your mind?' he asked quietly,
and she had the feeling that her answer now was more
important than anything that had gone before.

'Because I love you,' she said simply. 'Because sometimes it's more important to trust your instincts than
your reason. I realised I'd let my own jealousy blind me
to the facts. It's an awful thing, jealousy. It feeds on its
own mistakes.'

'Oh, Rachel...'

With a convulsive movement, his hand gripped her
jaw, turning her face to his. Then, with infinite ten-
derness, he brought her mouth to his, kissing her so
sweetly, it was like a benediction.

'I'm sorry,' she whispered, feeling the tears on her
cheeks and, feeling them, too, he used his tongue to lick
them away.

'All I'm sorry about is that it's taken you so long to
come to your senses,' he confessed huskily. 'You're my

only reason for living, Rachel. You—and Daisy. You're my life.'

Some time later, Rachel stirred amid the tumbled covers of her bed. She didn't quite remember how she came to be up there, except that Ben had been kissing her, and she seemed to recall him picking her up and carrying her upstairs...

And yes, she thought languorously, she remembered what had happened after that very well. Remembered his concern that he shouldn't hurt her, and her eagerness to assure him that he wouldn't. Remembered his undressing her, and caressing her, and how grateful she had been that her clothes had peeled off so easily, and then driving her half crazy with his hands and lips and tongue.

A wave of remembered bliss swept over her as she also remembered undressing him. Some things were never forgotten, and only her trembling fingers had turned a drama into a crisis. She smiled.

But then, he had made love to her—urgently, mindlessly at first, and then unhurriedly, leisurely, sharing the pleasure with her, teaching her again how magical it could be. Their lovemaking had been many things: wild, and tender; studied, and instinctive; a sensual supplication of the body, and a glorious celebration of the senses.

She stretched, and as she did so she became aware of the arm that was lying possessively across her breasts, and the hairy thigh wedged so confidingly between hers. Even in sleep, Ben's instincts were to keep her close to him, and she turned her head on the pillow to find he was also awake.

And, curiously, she felt a momentary sense of embarrassment. It was so long since he had seen her like this, totally naked and open to his gaze. But when she groped for the sheet, his hand prevented her, and propping himself up on one elbow, he looked down at her with tender eyes.

'Don't,' he said softly. 'Let me look at you. You know you're beautiful, don't you? So soft, and pink, and delicious.'

'And fat,' said Rachel ruefully, but she made no further attempt to cover herself. When he looked at her like that, all her inhibitions slipped away, and she could almost believe it herself.

'You're not fat,' he assured her, bending his head to take one dusky nipple in his mouth. His hands slid possessively over her stomach. 'I wouldn't have you any other way.'

Rachel trembled. 'Would—would you have come back if I hadn't had the fall?' she ventured huskily, and Ben lifted his head to give her a retiring look.

'Once I found out you weren't going to marry Barrass, you mean?' he asked drily. 'What do you think?'

'I hoped you would,' she admitted, with a shy smile. Then, as his hand dipped erotically between her legs, she hurried on, before her emotions got the better of her. 'Why—why did you take me to Watersmeet?' His probing fingers caused her to catch her breath. 'Did you think I'd remember the Armstrongs' name?'

Ben sighed, but he allowed her a moment's breathing space as he said, 'Well, you did, didn't you? Isn't that why you came to the hotel?'

'No.' Rachel was indignant now. 'I told you. I came to the hotel because I believed you. I didn't even think about the Armstrong thing, until I found Elena's photograph a few days later.'

Ben frowned. 'Her photograph? I didn't know we had a photograph of her.'

'Well, we did,' said Rachel firmly, loving the way he said 'we' so naturally. 'She sent us one, when she answered our advertisement. Don't you remember? She was standing outside the house.'

'What house? Oh—you mean Watersmeet.'

'Yes.'

'God.' Ben shook his head. 'I'd forgotten. And that's when you remembered? Well, well. Did it make a difference?'

'Only to me,' said Rachel ruefully, stroking her hand along his cheek. 'I was sure you'd never forgive me. But that was why you took me to the house, wasn't it?'

'Well, I had intended to say a lot more that evening,' he conceded. 'But then I told you that. I didn't dream we might get any further. I'd forgotten what a sexy creature you are.'

'Me?' Rachel laughed, but it was a soft contented sound. 'It's not the adjective that instantly springs to my mind.'

'Well, it does to mine,' Ben assured her thickly. 'Now stop talking. We've got better things to do.'

Rachel couldn't help it. A helpless wave of desire was sweeping over her again, and when he moved to lie between her legs her arms slid eagerly about his neck. Need, hot and passionate, was pulsing through her body, and she wound her legs about him as her senses took control.

It was as the heady after-shocks were dying away again that she thought of Daisy. 'What time is it?' she exclaimed, realising they must have been here for a couple of hours or more, and Ben obediently examined his watch.

'It's nearly half-past six, and yes, Karen will be bringing Daisy back fairly shortly. But don't worry, she has a key. I gave her one, in case I had to take you to a doctor.'

Rachel gasped. 'You mean, she could come in, and——'

'Well, we are married,' Ben reminded her drily. 'And before you ask, I had a couple of duplicate keys made while your mother was staying here.'

Rachel shook her head. 'Her suggestion, I suppose.'

'As a matter of fact, it was.'

'Oh, Ben!' She wound her arms around his neck. 'What am I going to do with you?'

'Take me back, I hope,' said Ben modestly. 'I haven't written a word since you told me you wanted a divorce. And as I was serious about buying a larger house in the district, I think you should help me to get over this writer's block!'

Auckland Harbour was actually two harbours: the Waitemata, and the Manukua. Dominating Waitemata harbour was a long island, called Rangitoto, and Ralph had told Rachel that no matter which angle you viewed it from it always looked the same.

The city itself, like Rome, was built on seven hills, although in Auckland's case they were actually seven or more extinct volcanoes. And, as New Zealand's largest city, it was also very cosmopolitan, enjoying its reputation as one of the cultural capitals of the Southern Hemisphere.

Rachel had been enchanted with it; enchanted, too, by her new stepfather and his generosity. She and Ben and Daisy had been made to feel very much at home and even baby Jaime's crying hadn't fazed his step-grandfather a bit.

Jaime's birth had been, to Rachel, one of the most magical events in a magical year. Contrary to those other occasions, when she had worried herself sick about having another baby, this time she had scarcely known she was pregnant at all until she felt their son move inside her. It had been an easy pregnancy, an easy birth; but it had delayed their visit to see Rachel's mother and brother in New Zealand. Now, with Jaime almost three months old, and a new book for Ben to promote in the bookshops, it seemed an ideal time for them to combine business with pleasure. And it had been mostly pleasure, Rachel thought, as she watched her husband get out of bed one cool April morning, and draw back the curtains. Pleasure—and an aching sense of immutability; a feeling of permanence that nothing could ever mar.

The view from their bedroom windows was quite spectacular, though Ben, shivering a little, came eagerly back to bed. But the fact that Ralph's house was built into the hillside overlooking the harbour meant every room had its own charm, and there was no doubt they'd miss it when they got back to London.

They were going home in two days, back to London first, then to the house Ben had bought in Wiltshire. They still owned the house in Upper Morton but they'd rented it to Cyril, since the fire department had insisted he couldn't live on the shop premises any longer. No one had ever found out who reported the old antiques dealer to the authorities. But Mr O'Shea had a wicked grin whenever the subject was mentioned.

'Will you be sorry to go back to England?' Ben asked now, warming his cold toes on her calves, and she shook her head tolerantly.

'Going home?' she asked, making the distinction. 'No, I won't be sorry to go home. I'll miss Mum and Ralph, of course, and David and his family, but they'll be coming over to visit later in the year. And I know Karen is dying to see the baby again. It's time Daisy went back to her lessons, too.' She smiled. 'I know she can't wait to tell her friends all about her new baby brother. And she'll be starting at her new school in the autumn.'

Daisy had been very pragmatic about the new arrival. She had treated the baby with an air of pride, mixed with a definite flavour of conceit. She considered she had played no small part in bringing her mother and father back together, and she maintained she'd known all along that it was bound to happen.

Rachel wished she had been so certain, but she let her daughter enjoy her moment of glory. It didn't matter how she and Ben had breached the gulf that had divided them. The important thing was that they had, and she'd never been as happy in her life.

'Mmm,' Ben murmured now, evidently pleased with her response. 'And what about you? Will you be eager to start work again, now that Jaime's old enough to be left with a nursemaid?'

Rachel pulled a wry face. 'No,' she replied carefully, knowing he still found talking about Elena's intrusion into their lives painful. She'd told him what Simon had said about the girl and Harry Armstrong, and sometimes, she knew, Ben felt a little bitter at all the time they'd wasted. But only sometimes. Those times were getting less and less frequent. Nevertheless, she had no intention of doing anything that might hurt him ever again, and looking after Jaime was still very much a full-time affair.

'I wouldn't mind, you know,' he said softly, as if he had read her mind, and she guessed how much it had cost him to say that.

Turning to him, she wrapped her arms around him. 'I would,' she assured him firmly. 'At least for the immediate future. Besides, we used to say we wanted four children when Daisy was a baby. Have we abandoned that ambition? Or do you need some time to think about it?'

Ben chuckled. He didn't.

Harlequin invites you to the most
romantic wedding of the season.

Rope the cowboy of your dreams in
Marry Me, Cowboy!

A collection of 4 brand-new stories,
celebrating weddings, written by:

New York Times **bestselling author**

JANET DAILEY

and favorite authors

Margaret Way
Anne McAllister
Susan Fox

Be sure not to miss Marry Me, Cowboy!
coming this April

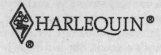 **HARLEQUIN®**

HARLEQUIN®

Deceit, betrayal, murder

Join Harlequin's intrepid heroines, India Leigh
and Mary Hadfield, as they ferret out the truth
behind the mysterious goings-on in their
neighborhood. These two women are no milk-
and-water misses. In fact, they thrive on

MISCHIEF & MAYHEM

Watch for their incredible adventures in this
special two-book collection. Available in March,
wherever Harlequin books are sold.

HARLEQUIN®

PRESENTS: *Plus*

Lindsey and Tim Ramsden were married—but, these days, in name only. Their once-passionate relationship hadn't survived a bitter misunderstanding, and they were separated by time and the Atlantic Ocean. Now Lindsey had another chance at happiness; could she accept that her marriage was finally over, and that it was time to move on?

"The first man to walk through this door will be the one I date for a month...." And he turned out to be Leo Kozakis—the man who had cruelly rejected Jacy ten years before! The sensible thing would be to forget the wager, but Jacy was seized by another reckless impulse: she was more than a match now for Leo—and she would seize her chances for passion...and revenge!

Presents Plus is Passion Plus!

Coming next month:

The Wrong Kind of Wife by Roberta Leigh
Harlequin Presents Plus #1725

and

Gamble on Passion by Jacqueline Baird
Harlequin Presents Plus #1726

Harlequin Presents Plus
The best has just gotten better!

Available in March wherever Harlequin books are sold.

PPLUS22-R

On the most romantic day of the year, capture the thrill of falling in love all over again—with

Harlequin's

Bachelors

They're three sexy and *very single* men who run very special personal ads to find the women of their fantasies by Valentine's Day. These exciting, passion-filled stories are written by bestselling Harlequin authors.

Your Heart's Desire by Elise Title
Mr. Romance by Pamela Bauer
Sleepless in St. Louis by Tiffany White

Be sure not to miss Harlequin's Valentine Bachelors, available in February wherever Harlequin books are sold.

HARLEQUIN®

VB

If you are looking for more titles by

ANNE MATHER

Don't miss these fabulous stories by one of
Harlequin's most distinguished authors:

Harlequin Presents®

#11354	INDISCRETION	$2.75	☐
#11444	BLIND PASSION	$2.89	☐
#11492	BETRAYED	$2.89	☐
#11542	GUILTY	$2.89	☐
#11553	DANGEROUS SANCTUARY	$2.89	☐
#11591	TIDEWATER SEDUCTION	$2.99	☐
#11617	SNOWFIRE	$2.99	☐
#11663	A SECRET REBELLION	$2.99 U.S.	☐
		$3.50 CAN.	☐
#11697	STRANGE INTIMACY	$2.99 U.S.	☐
		$3.50 CAN.	☐

(limited quantities available on certain titles)

TOTAL AMOUNT	$
POSTAGE & HANDLING	$
($1.00 for one book, 50¢ for each additional)	
APPLICABLE TAXES*	$_____
TOTAL PAYABLE	$_____
(check or money order—please do not send cash)	

To order, complete this form and send it, along with a check or money order
for the total above, payable to Harlequin Books, to: **In the U.S.:** 3010 Walden
Avenue, P.O. Box 9047, Buffalo, NY 14269-9047; **In Canada:** P.O. Box 613,
Fort Erie, Ontario, L2A 5X3.

Name: _____

Address: _____ City: _____

State/Prov.: _____ Zip/Postal Code: _____

*New York residents remit applicable sales taxes.
 Canadian residents remit applicable GST and provincial taxes.   HAMBACK3

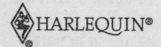

HARLEQUIN®